THE COWARD DOES
IT WITH A KISS

The Coward Does It With A Kiss

Rohase Piercy

The original edition of this book was published in 1990 by
The Gay Men's Press

The Raven's Book Bunker
www.theravensbunker.com

Cover Design by Charlie Raven

From *The Ballad of Reading Gaol*
by Oscar Wilde:

Yet each man kills the thing he loves,
By each let this be heard;
Some do it with a bitter look,
Some with a flattering word.
The coward does it with a kiss,
The brave man with a sword!

PREFACE

Much has been discovered about Constance Wilde's life since this book was first published in 1990. Franny Moyle's excellent 2011 biography *Constance – the Tragic and Scandalous Life of Mrs Oscar Wilde* drew on previously unpublished letters, as did Lexi Wolfe's 2016 one-woman play *Mrs Oscar Wilde*, and I'm grateful to both authors for the inspiration their work has provided. In addition, prestigious medical journal *The Lancet* published, in 2015, a retrospective diagnosis of the illness that plagued Constance on and off for the last ten years of her life – it is now believed that she was suffering from Multiple Sclerosis, a recognised but little understood condition in the late nineteenth century.

For this edition, I have tried to be wisely selective in incorporating new material into the narrative; I did not want to clog the flow of Constance's retrospection with new facts and dates unnecessarily, especially if they would have had no major impact upon her thoughts and feelings during her final months. I did feel, however, that two major characters in her story had not been given their full due in the original version, and felt honour bound to make amends. The first is Lady Georgina Mount-Temple, whom Constance's letters reveal to have been not only a wise and supportive friend, but also a second mother, a spiritual guide, and a trusted confidante as regards her marriage troubles. The second is Arthur Humphreys, manager of Hatchards Bookstore, whose love affair with Constance during the year leading up to Oscar's trial and disgrace I have now presented as consummated – letters written in 1894 in which she she addresses him as 'My darling Arthur' and speaks of her happiness at his having 'come into [her] life to fill it with love' giving me, I hope, sufficient licence to do so.

I have retained my own invented repercussions of this relationship as regards Oscar's downfall, and I have been careful to preserve the central theme of Constance's retrospective search for a handle on her own identity as she examines and re-examines her actions, reactions, motives, suspicions and above all her unconscious awareness of her husband's sexuality. I hope that the narrative still offers a plausible picture of what Constance Wilde might have been thinking, feeling and wanting to say during the last three months of her life.

Rohase Piercy
Brighton, 2019

Following her husband's imprisonment for gross indecency in May 1895, Constance Wilde fled with their two young sons Cyril and Vyvyan to the Continent.

She had less than three years to live.

She divided her time between Switzerland, where her brother Otho Holland Lloyd lived with his second family at Bevaix; Germany, where she enrolled her sons in school at Heidelberg and enjoyed the support of her expatriate friends Carlos and Carrie Blacker; and Nervi on the Italian Riviera, where she finally settled near her friend Lady Margaret Brooke, estranged wife of the English Rajah of Sarawak.

She was no longer known, of course, as Mrs Oscar Wilde; she had formally changed her name, and that of her sons, to one already adopted by her brother some years ago in an attempt to avoid his creditors.

She was now Constance Mary Holland.

Villa Elvira,
Bogliasco,
Nervi.

2nd of January 1898

My Dear Oscar,

You may be surprised to receive another letter from me so soon after my last, and indeed I had not intended to write again for I have nothing in particular to say that has not been covered by our recent correspondence. I'm sure I need hardly add that I have not changed my mind about anything, especially after your last letter to me, which is the letter of a madman. I suppose that A.D. is still with you? I hear rumours that Lady Q. has written to him, and that you are both short of money. I can only say that I hope she has withdrawn his allowance as I have withdrawn yours, and when I think of your going back to him after all that has happened, and then blaming *me* because I have been biding my time before inviting you here to join me, a thing which everyone agreed to be the most sensible and delicate course of action, I hope you may both starve.

Oscar, I will start again.

I do not want to write you another letter full of bitterness and recrimination. I want to write you at least one honest piece of correspondence, not to lecture you about your situation, but to tell you something about mine. Or are you so far steeped in the madness of self-pity that you have not even the imagination to see that your wife has a soul to be tormented also, a soul as precious as yours perhaps?

It is no use. I am so full, so saturated with bitterness and spite, that it appears I can neither speak nor write without barbs. I sometimes wonder whether my ill health is not caused by sheer anger - spite and resentment running like electricity through my nerves - which would account, perhaps, for the shooting pains and the tingling. Of course I have plenty of encouragement from my family and from well-meaning friends (and *your* well-meaning friends have done little to help the situation) – but encouragement is no excuse. The truth is that I am an unpleasant person masquerading as a likeable one, a vindictive woman pretending to be a martyr; one who chose with eyes wide open to go where I would seem to have been led innocent and blind. I say this in cold blood and without self-abasement; and I know that it will be as great a surprise to you as anyone, to know that I have long had a window through which to look into the secret recesses of your heart.

It has often been said to me (how often!) that I could not be blamed for having misunderstood you, that your actions were, and still are, beyond the comprehension of decent people. But I do understand you, Oscar; I understand you perfectly well. It is myself, myself I do not understand.

Cyril went back to Neuenheim yesterday, and I do miss him; especially as today is my birthday, as you know, and I enter my forty-first year. But it is a beautiful morning here at Nervi, and I feel quite well for the first time in days. Maria woke me with a breakfast tray on which lay a bouquet of sun-coloured roses – a gift from the Ranee, who always remembers me. She must have sent for them specially, at this time of year. Feeling rested, I rose early and have been sitting for some time now by my window, from which I can see the jasmine in bloom, and the white road leading down to the village. I have been leafing through an old diary which I found in the bottom of my trunk - I am still in the process of unpacking, you see! - and which I am very thankful to have kept by me, for I blush to think what the bailiffs who ransacked Tite Street would have made of it. I am not sure just what has prompted such a restrospective indulgence, at a time when retrospection can bring me nothing but pain – intimations of mortality, perhaps, having reached the age of forty (still young, the Ranee says, but it feels so old!); my ill health, et cetera; and thoughts of other birthdays, with you.

You think this a rambling and self-indulgent preamble, no doubt. Well, you should know all about that.

No. If I cannot do better than this, this letter had best not be sent at all. I am getting too tired, Oscar, to nag you for much longer, you will be relieved to hear. Would you be interested, I wonder, in what I have been reading?

Well, prepare yourself. The young woman who expressed herself thus was twenty-six years of age, and newly married; a young woman of artistic pretensions, ardent disciple of the Aesthetic Movement, and forty-eight hours wife of one who was, at the time, regarded as its High Priest.

Hotel Wagram, Rue de Rivoli

31st of May, 1884

The first day of my new life! And my first chance to write about it. It still seems like a wonderful dream, from which I pray I may never wake. I have a few hours to myself this morning – by choice, of course, for O. pressed me to join them in a morning stroll but I declined, thinking how delicious it would be to spend some time writing by the window in our room. We have a wonderful view of the Tuileries, and everything is in bloom, and I can see couples out strolling arm in arm just as O. and I did yesterday (as man and wife! How strange, and yet how completely natural it seems already to think of ourselves in those terms). Mr Sherard addressed me this morning as "Mrs Oscar"...

Oh, I forgot to mention that Robert Sherard arrived at breakfast this morning, and was introduced to me, and was altogether most charming and congratulatory. I had heard much about him from O. and so was very interested to meet him; he does not seem on first acquaintance to display any of the "puritanism" that O. likes to complain of – on the contrary, he seems a rather romantic figure, and puts me in mind of Chatterton. And he is the great-grandson of Wordsworth! Anyway, he and Oscar are taking a stroll together, and I do not at all begrudge them one another's company, for now I have a little solitude in which to revel in my happiness. To tell the truth, I am also feeling tired – and aching in every limb! I am very glad of those talks with Mama Mary back in Dublin, otherwise I might not be quite sure that all is as it should be (at least I have a grandmother I can talk to about these things! I could never have broached the subject with Mama!) It feels rather like one's monthly "indisposition", but it is not at all unpleasant; in fact I feel extremely smug and contented, and I shall never allow myself to be intimidated by a bitter old spinster like Aunt Emily again! For what does she know of life, when all is said and done?

"More happy love, more happy, happy love,
Forever warm, and still to be enjoyed,
Forever panting and forever young!"
(O. prefers Keats to Shelley, and I am coming round to his way of thinking - we read this aloud only last night, and laughed for pleasure!)
"Forever may I love, and he be fair!"

O. seems vastly pleased with himself, and enjoys

showing much tenderness and concern. I do not like to spoil it for him, although he knows perfectly well that I was neither ignorant - how could I be, with a father whose indiscretions were the talk of the household? - nor apprehensive! He insists that all his past experience counts for nothing, that there was no-one to compare to me, and of course that pleases me. And he is so beautiful ... I nearly told him what Lady M.B. said to me about the Rajah on her wedding night, but feared that instead of amusing him it might offend. His delicacy is so delightful, I hope he never loses it ...

Oh, Oscar! I really think I had better *not* send this letter. Embittered and cynical as I have become, it still brings an indulgent smile to my lips, even a nostalgic tear or two. And Robert Sherard! Not that I have any particular suspicions, for it is true that he was infected with a lingering puritanism ... but even so, more than one of my friends thought it strange, on the second day of our honeymoon, and said so! Well, it comes as no surprise to me now, to remember that I thought the two of you charming together. But see what comes next:

I am interrupted by a knock at the door, and there has just been delivered a beautiful bouquet from O., who has not yet been gone more than an hour and a half, and a card with sweet words on it! What must Mr Sherard think of us?

(What indeed? I remember how, a few days later,

10

he threatened to throw his swordstick out of the carriage door on the grounds of being tempted to murder us for being too happy. I thought it a great joke, and offered to relieve him of the tempting weapon there and then...)

Ah, Oscar, our honeymoon! Visits to John Donaghue's studio (you remember the bas-relief of the naked boy harpist we both admired so much?); Sarah Bernhardt's wonderful Lady Macbeth; ordering heaps of new clothes (*at last* I could order with impunity the costumes of which Aunt Emily so disapproved - soft flowing fabrics, rich colours, no bustle); reading Keats to one another in the evenings, when "Chatterton" had made his bow and retired. And we were in Paris, in June! Of all places and all seasons! I felt as though a banner had unfurled in my heart declaiming *Liberté, égalité, fraternité!* Strolling through the Tuileries in the evening, lamps flaring out against an indigo sky - I felt like a queen newly crowned, installed in the palace of your heart, Oscar, with all your adorers hastening to cast themselves at my feet also.

After Paris, Dieppe was quiet, was it not? A little too quiet for you, I think, but for me it was just what I wanted, for I needed time to reflect, and prepare for our return to London. I had much to reflect on – at least, I seem to have thought so at the time, for my diary entries become quite copious, all much in the same rapturous vein:

Oscar is like the white moon, hiding the secret blue of his eyes under langorous heavy lids, and the amber waves of his hair are like an aureola around him. He makes me feel as deep and as powerful as the sea; the moon leans down, and she rocks him in her lap, like a lover.

A little too "utter", perhaps, but not all bad I think – even comparable to something of yours? I was told that you described me on occasion as a "violet-eyed Artemis" - well, I cannot imagine that you found me much like Artemis on our honeymoon! Looking back, I wonder whether I might even have frightened you a little?

Received today a letter from Lady Wilde, who addresses me as "Dearest Constance" and signs herself "La Madre Devotissima"! Mainly compliments about the wedding... Will I ever live up to her expectations? I wish I had the courage to display even half her unconventionality! I really do not want to be a Virgilia to her Volumnia, though I am sometimes afraid that is how people will see us.

Ah, poor Speranza. She was looking for a daughter to fill the chasm left by your little sister's death all those years ago. I think that in time I did come to fill it, at least partly. I certainly did come to love her, with a true affection; it is one of my greatest regrets that I was not more of a comfort and support to her at the last.

Nervi
9th of January 1898

And now a week has elapsed. I was obliged to break off my writing by a surprise visit from the Ranee who came to wish me a happy birthday, so sweet of her! We spoke much about the old days, my mind having been set on a retrospective train of thought … we spoke of you, Oscar. She compared you to Humpty Dumpty, "who fell and could not rise again" … and all the King's horses, and all the King's men … I have heard nothing from you in the meantime, so I suppose all is as it was. I was, alas, a little too optimistic about my health last week, and have been laid up for the last few days though I am a little better now. I am using the typewriter as you see, because it is so painful for me to write longhand. I have made up my mind that I *will* go to Genoa for that operation. I do not want to become a permanent invalid, which is what I very nearly am at times. Carrie Blacker recommends the operation, and truly I can see that I have little to lose by it.

But I shall wait until after next month, when I will have seen Vyvyan! We missed him at Christmas – but he was, by all accounts, very keen to stay and take part in the ceremonies. He seems very happy with the Jesuits, Oscar - something I know would

13

not upset *you*, though Adrian Hope is rather
disapproving. I should not say this, but there are
times when I think that he was not the ideal choice
of guardian for our boys. He has little sympathy for
children, it seems, and ours need so much sympathy
and understanding just now … in any case, since he
hardly sees them I suppose it hardly signifies.
Everyone says it will do them no harm to have a
conservative influence, and the Hopes, try as they
might (and in the early days they did try, as you will
remember!) just cannot be anything other than
conservative. We used to enjoy shocking them,
didn't we, when we first launched ourselves upon
London society? We predicted a very dull married
life for them, in comparison with ours.

To tea with the Troubridges. Laura made several
pointed remarks about the boldness of the
aesthetic costume, how it displays the contours of
the figure when lacking a bustle and so on, which I
of course ignored. She professes to be *absolument
ravie* with us, our marriage and our plans for the
future, but I sense disapproval and maybe a hint of
jealousy. She is of course a former disciple of O.'s
who has fallen by the wayside. What a vicious little
pointed chin she has!

That was in the July of 1884, after our return to
London. We were staying, I think, at Great College
Street while our House Beautiful was gradually
taking shape – I sometimes feared it would never be
anything more than a castle in the air, it took so
long! I do not recall whether Miss Laura

Troubridge was yet entertaining any ambitions to become Mrs Adrian Hope, but he was certainly waiting in the wings for his cue …

You see I have been continuing my perusal of these old diaries. I have also been re-reading this letter, and I wonder whether I have not been a little hard on myself; there is much to learn from one's own words of nearly a decade and a half ago! There cannot be many people, I suppose, who find the spectres of their youth endearing … but I will try to suspend judgement of the new Mrs Wilde for the moment. She holds the key to my present identity.

(Identity! That is precisely what I seem to have so little of in my own right – it is all bound up with yours. I do not speak of *character* – that which the world says you have lost, Oscar, and cannot redeem – one's character is what one makes it, what one continues to make it. But *identity* – at least you have one! And by "you" I mean not only *you,* Oscar, but all your friends, all your kind, even down to the likes of Alfred Taylor. As you were so fond of telling me, you have a history. In spite of everything, you have a sense of pride - you think I did not know this? - and you have the language to describe *who you are*; whereas I - who am I?)

Of course I would never have dreamt of asking such a question when we eventually moved into our house in Tite Street on my twenty-seventh birthday! I was "Mrs Oscar Wilde", and the Press soon bestowed upon me another title: "Châtelaine of the House Beautiful". Saddened though I was by my grandfather's death, and impatient with your long absences ("civilising the provinces" with your lectures), I was eager to take up my role as the happiest woman in London.

15th of January, 1885

Too sick to leave my room today, although it is a beautiful morning, very mild for January, with soft sunlight at the window and birdsong in the trees outside ... the colours of my room glow blue, ivory and gold ... all is tranquil, except for my heaving stomach! I half descended earlier, but the smell of breakfast cooking rose up from the basement and compelled me to beat a hasty retreat. How long can it go on? Aunt Mary Napier assures me that it should soon be passing, but Lady Wilde says that her sickness lasted the whole nine months on each occasion, and that she was never so miserable in all her life, though the great joy afterwards was ample compensation. I am sure that this latter will prove true, but if it goes on like this I don't see how I am to bear it. It is not just the nausea, but the overwhelming weariness and heaviness of limb that accompanies it. Perhaps if it were possible to "put on a good face" I should not mind so much – but my skin is so blotched, and my eyelids so swollen, that I despair of myself everytime I cross in front of the glass.

O. has been most solicitous as always, and himself brought me a tray with tea and bread and butter, which I was able to eat. But he was obliged to go out, and I did not wish to keep him. He goes away again next week. I must try to keep cheerful. I know that he hates to leave me at such a time.

Well, I will not embarrass you further, Oscar, for actually I knew a good deal better than that, though obviously I did not wish to believe it. You found me disgusting, and were relieved to be away from me, though you tried not to show it and I pretended not to know. Dissembling was never your strong point, you know; I was always much better at it than you were.

Would you like to know when I first realised that your feelings towards me were going to change? Cast your mind back, if you can, to one of your mother's salons in Oakley Street – I have only to close my eyes, and I can see it all so clearly. It is late autumn. As always, the curtains are drawn and the room dimly lit by candles, although it is but three o'clock in the afternoon. The room is crowded, and looks more so because the huge mirrors give the illusion of double the space, double the number of people. You and I, or course, are used to this – newcomers are usually somewhat overwhelmed.

The air is heavy with incense and I have a headache. Too listless to seek out companionship of my own, I remain at your side, watching your mother hold court in the centre of the room. She is being "Speranza, Hope of the Nation" - the nation in question being Ireland, naturally - resplendent in swathes of lace and velvet, with an impressive array

of necklaces at her throat and a large brooch fixed
into the centre of her turban-like headdress. Her
jewels wink in the candle light. No-one raises an
eyebrow at her eccentric appearance - surrounded
by her acolytes, she holds magnificent sway. I
know of no other hostess who could get away with
it. How pale, silly and insignificant we young girls
appear beside such a matriarch! I am always so
afraid of being laughed at ... With half an ear I am
aware of your conversation with Arthur Balfour,
who has strolled over to join us. Beauty appears to
be the subject yet again. I have heard you hold
forth many times on the aesthetic ideal – many
times, but not yet too often – we are not yet six
months married.

"It is the Attic form," you say, "that shows
physical beauty at its ideal; those graceful, athletic
boys, those slim demure girls; the simple lines of
the tunic following the natural lines of the figure,
with none of these pendulous furbelows, these huge
swellings grossly accentuated, which rob the figure
of its lightness and purity. In women especially, the
pursuit of beauty should demand as simple a style
as possible. A youthful, almost boy-like form is the
ideal, and any additions, any intimations of gross
physicality, should be disguised rather than
accentuated. That is what women of the modern
age would do well to make their golden rule."

Our companion smiles, a trifle bemused. His gaze
slides towards your mother – he cannot help it.

"I think you may have difficulty in convincing the
female population at large, Oscar," he says mildly,
"perhaps your wife might have better success, if she

cares to undertake the task; she exhibits so beautifully those qualities which you have just described, and most women baulk at taking fashion advice from their menfolk."

Finding myself thus drawn into the conversation, I smile and incline my head.

"Oh, Constance is a Hebe amongst the nymphs," you concur with enthusiasm, "she often designs her clothes herself, did you know? Slim, straight lines, you see, following the natural fall of the material; and if there are to be puffs, let them be only in the sleeve."

Poor Mr Balfour appears embarrassed as he follows your descriptive gesture. I laugh lightly, to put him at his ease, though I am not feeling easy myself – less so as I remember why.

"Why, as to that, I think women should dress to be *comfortable*," I say; "and what seems suitable at one stage of a woman's life may not necessarily remain so at the next. The "slim, demure" impression of which Oscar is so fond suits the younger woman – one might almost say that its charm is the charm of immaturity."

"Come, come Constance! You do yourself a disservice!" You are surprised; more than surprised, displeased, I can feel it. This is the first time I have ever challenged your opinion in public.

"That was not my intention, Oscar," I say calmly. "I merely wished to make the obvious point that my style of dress, which looks well at the age of twenty-seven, may not suit me so well at forty-seven. Look around the room! How many women do you see who have the youthful, boylike figure of which you speak? What age are they? I hope you do not think that those who are more mature, more voluptuous or statuesque, are *ipso facto* not beautiful? Look at your own mother!"

Mr Balfour nods enthusiastically. You, however, make a sharp gesture of annoyance.

"My mother is a Juno amongst the goddesses, and a true matriarch is always an exception. What are you talking of, Constance? There is room for only one Juno among many Daphnes. My mother is a figurehead, an Olympian queen. But you cannot expect me to believe, my dear, that a Hebe such as yourself would not consider it a tragedy to lose those graceful lines, that youthful slimness, to become bloated and grotesque like a hippopotamus?"

"Well, of course I do not wish to become bloated and grotesque, Oscar, but I will not always retain the figure of a young girl. There are – developments in every women's life, you know, and her style of beauty should surely reflect this ..."

I cannot be more specific, in company. But you are annoyed, and totally oblivious.

"Yes, yes, of course my dear, but I hope *your* developments will never lead you in *that* direction, for instance." You point out an unfortunate lady, short and plump and dressed in a low-cut gown with prominent bustle, who is engaged in animated discourse with her friends, happily innocent of the attention bestowed upon her.

"She resembles nothing so much as a bunch of grapes! Now where is the beauty in that?"

"There *is* beauty, Oscar -" I say, but am too upset

to continue. I find myself flushing angrily at the gratuity of the insult. Luckily we are joined at that point by another couple, and poor Mr Balfour is spared further embarrassment. A thin, angular woman whose name I must have immediately forgotten engages me in conversation, and I must keep my vexation to myself.

Beauty is Truth, Truth Beauty; that is all we know, and all we need to know. Our beloved Keats. You quoted those lines to me later that evening.

"You are my beauty, best beloved, and all my truth as well," you said, and kissed my eyes and mouth. I did not choose that moment to tell you that I was carrying our first child.

21st of January 1885

Did not leave the house today, but found plenty to occupy me and have been feeling most tranquil and contented because the sickness has eased a little. I have a sense of having taken root amongst all this ivory and sunlight. My roots go down through the house, through the foundations of the city, into the deep earth, tapping the hidden springs.

Lady W. is trying to encourage me to go out while O. is away, and I know I must make the effort – but I am happy here, tending the house like a priestess. My room has become a Holy of Holies – or maybe it is I who am the Holy of Holies, blessed as I am with a sacred presence within. Lady W. reminds me that "confinement" nowadays is not meant to encompass the whole of one's pregnancy! But I find I rather like the idea, it feels ancient and pure ...

Yes, it seems that I too, without realising it, was happier when you were away. And yet I convinced myself that I was desolate without you, that I longed for your company day and night – and that your tender courtesy towards me more than compensated for that tactful withdrawing of your passion which was, after all, but the manifestation of your delicacy, your respect for my condition.

But there was one occasion when you did manage to shock me, Oscar, and that occasion was our visit to Edward Heron-Allen, about three months before Cyril's birth. I remember that I was feeling particularly well that day, although the sickness never did quite leave me. We walked to Edward's lodgings, I leaning heavily upon your arm, and we debated on the way whether or not to ask him to prepare a horoscope when baby arrived. You chaffed me about Edward having proposed to me in Dublin – and I wondered, just for a moment, what my life would have been like if I had accepted him.

Anyway, we arrived, and as we stood at the door you whispered, "We will see whether he is still so smitten with you *now*!" It took me a few moments to work out what you meant, and then we were in the hall and the servant was taking our coats, and I had not time to show you how much your self-betrayal had hurt me.

Well, he was still "smitten", that is to say he was as affectionate and chivalrous towards me as ever, and I think that it piqued you to see it. We admired his wonderful rooms – his amazing violin collection, the dusty tomes on the mantelpiece, the astrological charts upon the walls, the heavy brocade curtains, the silk cushions, the incense, the dust! And he took great delight in showing and explaining to us some of the bizarre and extravagant objects he'd brought back from his foreign travels. There were knives and semi-precious stones, incense burners, and a few small statuettes in rough sandstone or terracotta which were not at all Attic! It was one of these which caught my eye, and I asked Edward to bring it over to me – I was seated upon the chaise-longue. He did so, very carefully, explaining that it was over three thousand years old, which made me too nervous to hold it and I begged him to lay it down upon the occasional table beside me. It was a representation of a naked woman, no more than four inches high, hugely swollen with pregnancy, almost spherical, supported on absurdly short legs while her small thin arms curved around to support her pendulous breasts. Her face also was small and insignificant, hardly thicker than her neck, the expression on it indecipherable because worn away by the years, though the nose jutted out sharply, like a beak.

I experienced a most powerful sensation, Oscar, as I looked at this image – as though the imaginary roots of which I had written earlier reached out from me to her, and drew from her the water of life. I felt my parched body drink it in thirstily, and I felt my baby move inside me as though aware of her numinous presence. I do not know how long I sat there transfixed; I was aroused by your wandering over to see what held my attention and making an angry, impatient, dismissive gesture.

"This is hideous! Whatever is it?" Your words, tiny and insignificant, dropped into the pool of aeons surrounding her.

"She is an image of the Earth Mother, most primitive of all divinities," replied Edward calmly. "I believe she hails from ancient Mesopotamia – most such idols do – but I came across this particular one in Morocco."

You coughed politely and turned away. "Well, thank heavens for the advent of civilisation! Really, it is too grotesque – Edward, *must* you have such monstrosities on display? Have you nothing beautiful to show me?"

And you discovered that he had, after all, a small replica of the *Apollo Belvedere* upon which you cast yourself with coos of delight and an enthusiasm exaggerated even for you - for you had, I think, been disturbed more deeply than you cared to admit by the obvious resemblance between the shape of my body, once beloved for its "boy-like slimness", and the "hideous, grotesque" image which stood before you on the table.

Nervi
21st of January 1898

I have been forgetting to date this letter. That last little apologia was actually written over two or three days. Now I read it through and find it self-indulgent, though it is a true record of my thoughts and feelings at the time. My state of mind slides from one extreme to another; how can I possibly write coherently about such an ephemeral subject as myself?

It is just as well that I have decided not to send this to you, Oscar. So many contradictory expressions would try your patience sorely. You could never bear hesitation or ambivalence in others – which is rather ironic, is it not, since when faced with your own terrible predicament you destroyed everything by your prevarication. However you would no doubt say that events at that time were out of your control, that you were not the captain of your destiny. I know who was, and it certainly was not Fate as you may like to suppose! How is he? You see, I try to avoid writing, as well as speaking, his abominable name. I have been hearing rumours that he has left you, though I do not yet know whether this is in fact the case. When I hear something definite, I may contact you.

But I do not think I will change my mind about

your allowance, since I know exactly what will happen if I let you have more money. I would be most happy to pay your hotel bill direct, if it were reasonable, and if I could be sure of your staying in one place. But you squander all the money that reaches you on drink, and other pleasures too no doubt.

The weather continues fine here, and believe it or not, there are already signs of Spring. Yesterday I went for a beautiful drive and saw buds on the trees! There are olive groves not far from here, Oscar – do you still wax romantic over olive groves? They used to make you speak of Gethsemane ... you often compared yourself to Christ, not overtly of course, but obliquely, with reference to His Passion ... strange, but I never thought it blasphemous. Nor do I now, I realise, in spite of everything.

I have definitely arranged to go to Monaco in three weeks' time, to see Vyvyan (I *must* get used to the new spelling – we all must – *Vivian*) and spend some time with him. It seems an age since I saw him – you would be pleased to know that he seems happy now, Oscar, he is not bullied at the Collegio as he was at Neuenheim and Freiburg. The Jesuits are kind, and the regime seems to suit him. He has a gentle nature still. He does not know what has happened to you, and I have to decide whether he is now ready to hear it. He is not yet twelve years old ... but then Cyril knew at ten, and broached the subject with me himself ... how can two brothers, so close in age, be so different?

Cyril is a brave boy, Oscar – you would be proud of him, he has the true Irish fighting spirit. You will have seen from the photograph I sent you that he has grown thinner in the face, and already looks quite grown up – he is tall for his age, which I see as a good thing for it means he is not easily bullied or intimidated. But I still miss the sweet baby he once was.

When I explained to him the meaning of the words he had read in the papers and seen on the billboards in the aftermath of your conviction, he did not show the least surprise - shall I tell you what he said? I have never repeated it to anyone, for one-one but yourself would think it innocent or touching.

"Oh! But I knew that Papa loves Bosie – didn't you know, Mama?"

I remember exactly where we were sitting, in the library at Tite Street. I do not know why I chose the library - I suppose I wanted somewhere more formal, less domestic - and *your* preserve. We sat by the fireplace, with no fire. I studied the carvings in the mantelpiece surround, the peacocks, the roses. I had to bite my tongue to prevent myself from asking – how did he know, when did he know, that he considered it something that went without saying? What had he seen, what had he heard? And where? At Babbacombe? At Worthing? What ideas had been taking root in his mind?

"Didn't *you* know, Mama?" He was persistent, and I had to reply.

"Yes; yes darling, I did know … but really, it is not something we ought to talk about -"

"And was that what made you cry so much? Was that what made you unhappy? Because I asked Papa, and he said he would rather die than make you unhappy, and that you should not be sad because he loved Bosie because it did not stop him from loving you, and it was a different kind of love, and I would understand when I was grown up. But do *you* understand, Mama?"

"I – understand, yes. I did understand."

What could I say? How could I protect him? How far had I failed to protect him already? You may well imagine, Oscar, what manner of thoughts were chasing through my mind. And there was something else, something I should not have felt, not admitted …

"But you must know, Cyril, that other people will *not* understand. Did you speak to anyone about it while you were in Dublin? Cousin Stanhope, for instance?'

"I tried to, Mama, but he would not tell me anything. He said it was a great shame that had come upon the family. That was why I thought it must be something terrible that Papa had done. Are you sure there is nothing else, Mama? Because I do not think Cousin Stanhope realises -"

"No – no, there is nothing else, Cyril." *Only more of the same, but I will spare you that.* "But what I am trying to tell you, darling, is that other people - our friends and relatives – will not want to hear you speak of Papa and Lord Alfred. You see – your Papa is a very special person -"

"I know. He told me so."

I could not repress a smile, but continued doggedly, "And special people often behave in an unusual way – a way that other people do not like, because they do not understand it. And that is why our friends will not like to hear about Papa and Lord Alfred. Because it is unusual. Unusual, that is, for a gentleman to – to love – that is, be in love with - another gentleman – and -"

"But it said in the paper that Papa had committed unnatural crimes!" Tears. Puzzlement. He was not listening to me.

"Yes, that is the way most people see it, Cyril, you might as well know that -"

"But everybody loves Papa! How could they say things like that about him?"

"Not everyone sees these things in the same way, darling -"

"But they are going to send him to prison! Mama, it isn't fair!"

"No, darling. It is not fair. We must be very brave."

"I love Papa! Do you love him, Mama? You do still love him, don't you?"

"I - yes, darling, I do. I do still love him."

"And he does still love us, doesn't he?"

"Of course he does. He will never stop loving you or your brother, Cyril, I am sure of that."

"And does Bosie still love him?"

Ah no! Never ask me that! How can I answer such a question? "We must hope so, Cyril."

"Are they going to send Bosie to prison too?"

"No – no, they will not send Lord Alfred to prison." *Stop now. I cannot speak of it any more. Please, please do not ask me any more.*

(*"And does Bosie still love him?"* How would I know? A strange sort of love it must be, that would drive the beloved into the arena and sit back to cheer on the spectacle...)

Yes, I felt utterly wretched, and in addition I felt
something else, half buried beneath all the suspicion
and guilt – a distinct twinge of jealousy. I was
jealous of my own unhappy son, jealous of his
innocence, of his easy acceptance of what the world
condemned – and, still more terrible, I was jealous
of his position with regard to you and your lover – a
beloved child, trusted, safe, not excluded because
not considered dangerous. I envied him those days
at Babbacombe about which I dared not inquire, I
envied him those boat trips at Worthing while I sat
at home listless and spiteful ...

"But I knew ... " and there was no guilt, no shame.
But he has learned since then, Oscar. I think it was
when we had to change our name that his innocence
was finally taken from him.

I told him – I told them both – that they must try to
forget that they had ever borne the name of Wilde.
I told them to practise their new signatures, practise
writing the name "Holland"; and Vivian had to
practise the new spelling of his Christian name. He
seemed to think it a game, not something to be
linked with you and your absence from our lives;
but Cyril – Cyril knew. He went and hid in the
summer house in Otho's garden, and refused to
come out for hours until I implored him, with tears,
to come into the house and eat some supper.

Carlos Blacker goes to Paris next month. If I had
your address, I would give it to him so that he could
come and visit you. I'm sure it would give you both
pleasure to see one another. And I would dearly

love to hear first-hand news of you, instead of rumour. If you would write to me again now, Oscar, I would answer.

Friday, 5th of June, 1885. You know the date by heart, Oscar, as I do. It was hot. That made it worse. Dr de Lacy and the midwife arrived at four in the afternoon. There was no-one else with me, for the only people I would have wanted were dear Mama Mary, who was in Dublin, and you, Oscar – and though you prided yourself on being the most modern of husbands I knew that this was something I could not ask of you.

But we managed very well. I took only a few drops of the chloroform, and when I came round and our firstborn son was placed in my arms – how can I describe what I felt? It was like being present at the creation of the world! To bring a whole new life into being – you men have no idea - it is a miracle, there is no other word for it! His thin, bleating cry set every nerve in my body a-tingle, and I looked down at his crumpled little face and knew that this moment, this great rush of love, would eclipse anything else I might achieve in the whole of my life. *Then* you came in, full of eagerness and apprehension, and we spent those first few hours in the delirium of joy and relief that all new parents know together.

And Oscar, you were the most delightful, the most tender of fathers, adored by your children, boasted of by your wife, admired by all our friends. We shared the distillation of sweetness that was Cyril, uncovering each day a deeper layer of tenderness towards him; it was like delving into a rainbow. The grasp of his soft little hand around a finger; his hungry mouth pursed into a round 'O', gradually giving way to the wide pink smiles with which he greeted us whenever we appeared in the nursery; and those long, serious, quizzical stares which you compared to the expression of a High Court Judge - though perhaps neither of us finds that particular analogy amusing any more. And of course, you were convinced that your son would be a genius, because he was born with a bridge to his nose!

Yes, those were wonderful days. Cyril ensnared our hearts with tendrils of love, and our lives without him seemed hollow in retrospect. You urged the joys of fatherhood upon all your friends, and Edward Heron-Allen produced a horoscope which we did not believe, saying our son was destined for a military career when you were determined that his feet should tread no path but that of Art.

Our financial troubles continued, of course – you were obliged to take on yet another lecture tour because we'd lost a considerable sum of money wrangling with Godwin's contractors over the work on our House Beautiful. I was not downhearted, however – on the contrary, I was full of plans and ideas! Nurse was marvellous with Cyril, and I felt so well, brimming over with pride and vigour, that I wanted to "branch out". My new role as society hostess, presiding over the "at homes" with which Mrs Oscar was expected to entice the brightest butterflies of London society to Tite Street, served only to whet my appetite. The wonderful women who graced our drawing-room - Mrs Langtry, Ellen Terry, Katharine Bradley and her other half, Marie Corelli – had not let the domestic grass grow under their feet, and neither should I! I considered the possibilities: I had enjoyed taking part in amateur productions such as *Helen in Troas* – might I perhaps go on the stage?

Well, I am heartily thankful that I never made such an amusing spectacle of myself as I undoubtedly would have done, had I carried that particular plan through! You were keen that I should be a second Mrs Langtry (I have never got over my annoyance, by the way Oscar, at the extent to which you idolised her); but as I remember pointing out to you at the time, I did not have the advantage of her particular footing with His Royal Highness! You thought it most indelicate of me to mention it.

Novel-writing was another option which attracted me – and in this I was encouraged by your mother, most generously given that I knew she would rather have me settle for the role of amanuensis to your talents. We spent long afternoons in discussion, arguing over the style of Victor Hugo, whom you did not admire ... and of course I never got beyond the first chapter. Instead I found myself shoehorned into the British Museum's reading room, researching articles on the history of fashion for you, or rather for the articles you promised to arrange for me with various newspapers.

But of course in the end it all came to naught, for by the time Cyril's first Birthday came around I had already retreated into the sanctuary of the home again, sick and swollen, with blotched complexion

and a resigned but sweet anticipation in my heart –
we hoped for a daughter this time, Isola Deirdre, a
grand Irish name suggested by your mother in
memory of your little sister who died so young.

25th of November, 1886

Today we went to register Vyvyan's birth! I have no
idea how we came to take so long about it – I really
did think O. had done it, after that argument we
had about the date. I still cannot see why the 5th of
November should be so very inauspicious – in fact I
have always suspected O. of harbouring a secret
admiration for the Catholic conspirators! But he is
very conscious at the moment of our family being in
the public gaze, and thinks it will do the Aesthetic
Movement a disservice to be associated with Guy
Fawkes Day, such nonsense! So 3rd of November is
the date we have given to the Registrar, and to our
friends we are saying that the days surrounding our
son's birth were such a whirlwind that we cannot
exactly remember on which of them he arrived – I
only hope they believe us!

But I remember, of course – it was the 5th of
November, and it was a much more protracted,
exhausting and painful business than had been the
case with Cyril. I was too fatigued, too confused by
the drugs, to hold him immediately, and when I
finally came to myself he had already been
inspected and named by his father.

Vyvyan Oscar Beresford Wilde (O. has completely

changed his mind about one Christian name being quite enough for any child – poor Cyril!) weighs only a little less than his brother did at birth, but it now seems incredible to think that Cyril was ever this tiny! Nurse brings him in to see his little brother every day; so far he has not been impressed. He dons his "judgely" expression and frowns at him without saying a word. Nurse assures us that all firstborns treat their new siblings so, and that he will come to adore Baby in time ...

Vyvyan has long, artistic fingers and thin little feet, and more hair than Cyril had, though it is lighter in colour. I think he is going to look more like his father – Cyril, I feel, favours me. O. does not gush over our little newcomer as he did over Cyril. I think that his disappointment over our not having produced Isola Deirdre is severe. Lady W. is consoling herself with the thought that we will reproduce her family, and have two boys first and then a daughter...

Oh dear – all this has had the effect of making me feel guilty about my own sense of relief. Of course it <u>would</u> have been nice to have a child of each sex, but I realise that I was – and still am – rather nervous of having a daughter. Everybody assures me that a daughter is the greatest comfort a mother can have, a friend and confidante for life – but this is certainly not the case between my mother and myself, and I would be so afraid of repeating the feeling that exists between us with a daughter of my own. I hesitate to name that feeling, for I can think of no other description for it than "mutual resentment". I think Mother has resented my presence in her life from the moment I was born, that in some way which I have never understood I spoilt everything for her. I suppose that is why she was so harsh with me as a child, why I had to endure all those public humiliations, all those private threats and scoldings. No wonder I was always ill! She pretends now that it never happened, of course. She and her husband sent a nicely worded telegram congratulating us on our son's birth, but she has not visited yet, nor has she seen Cyril in over six months ...

But I do wish that O. were not quite so distant towards the poor little mite, though I suppose Baby is too young for it to make any difference to him. O. jokes that he has let him down by having no bridge to his nose! I know it is not meant seriously, but it is a joke I cannot laugh at ... there is nothing wrong with Baby's nose...

I feel disproportionately upset that Mr Ruskin has declined to be godfather, though his excuses were made very nicely. O. now wants to ask Mortimer Menpes, whom I do not like very much, but I suppose he will do.

Oh! Speaking of Catholics (I mean my reference to the Gunpowder Plot conspirators earlier), we received a most kind note and a beautiful bouquet from young Robert Ross a couple of days ago. I did so enjoy meeting him in the summer, and the time he spent with us - his humour is quite infectious and brought me out of myself when I might otherwise have been feeling low. Also it was good for O. to have some lively company while I was indisposed with the pregnancy. I am glad he has made a friend of him. There is something so relaxed and affable about Robbie, as we call him, that sets me immediately at my ease ... he is different from other young men in that respect ... I wonder why?

Nervi
11th of February 1898

Oh, Oscar, I have just been reading the extracts
from your wonderful new poem in the *Daily
Chronicle*. It made me cry. I hear that it was only
published two days ago and has already sold out. I
have just been writing to Otho about it. I wonder
whether you will send me a copy? If not, I shall ask
Carlos Blacker to get hold of one for me. I may
even write to you. Yes, I will write to you.

Oscar, when I read your beautiful words I am
moved and thrilled as ever by your genius – and I
see in these lines your humanity, your tenderness,
shining through intact, inviolate in spite of all the
violations you have suffered. I feel so ashamed of
my bitterness, my pettiness and spite. Why can I
not "rise above the miasma of the commonplace",
as your mother always claimed to do? How am I to
judge what you have suffered, in prison and
elsewhere? And yet through it all you still had
compassion for a fellow prisoner, one whose
situation was more bleak, more desperate than your
own.

Some kill their love when they are young,
And some when they are old;
Some strangle with the hands of Lust
Some with the hands of Gold;
The kindest use a knife, because
The dead so soon grow cold.

For nearly three years, Oscar, I have tried to kill my love for you, telling myself that I had every reason, every duty even, to do so, trying to see as the world sees. But the poor corpse at my feet will not go cold, will not go still. Do you remember that I wrote to you, before we were married, that I had "no power to do anything but just love you"? It seems that I laid a curse upon myself then, from which I shall never be free. Every achievement of my life has now been compelled to bite the dust in the face of my association with you, and yet I still cannot say that I do not love you. How could it be otherwise, when the very thing which should make me hate you was that which also made me love you, even before I knew what it was? That is what I meant, Oscar, when I said that I understood you, but not myself.

No, I could not do the deed when I was young, and cannot do it now, when I feel so old. And I am not kind, I cannot do it quickly. That is why it is impossible for me to separate my life completely from yours, as so many have urged me to do.

It was not my love for you that I killed, Oscar, but that illusion, cherished for so long, that I could hold you captive to watch, like some exotic wild creature, and that your restless pacing was nothing more than the manifestation of a bright creative spirit. I strangled that illusion, along with any I may have had about *him*, when I realised at last that it was no longer a game, it was no longer charming to watch you with your beautiful young men, for this one was no mere plaything but a deadly and unscrupulous rival who meant to claim you for his very own, and could afford to pay an extravagant price to do so.

And then came that summer at Worthing, our last summer together with the children. He came to stay with us there, uninvited, and – well, you know what happened.

> *Yet each man kills the thing he loves,*
> *By each let this be heard,*
> *Some do it with a bitter look,*
> *Some with a flattering word.*
> *The coward does it with a kiss,*
> *The brave man with a sword!*

It is difficult to express quite what that summer meant to me; a terrible change came over me then, like losing one's innocence – though it is doubtful whether that is the right name for what I lost, for what I killed.

I hope the poem sells well, because it will mean money for you! And I hope that you will be encouraged by this success to write more. I would dearly love to hear that you have taken up your pen again, for if you could only apply yourself to producing more work like this, I truly think I could rebuild everything.

Nervi
14th of February 1898

Today I received my copy of the Ballad, with your note! I *knew* that you would send me one. I will treasure it dearly, and have been reading it through all morning. Thank you for telling me that you've also sent a copy to Otho – I'm glad that you recognise how good a brother-in-law he has been to you. You know he warned me against you, Oscar, before we married? He tried to give me some brotherly advice - referred to some scandal at Oxford - I didn't want to know. I never asked him for the details, not even afterwards, though I'm sure I can guess now. He's had scandals enough of his own, of course, over the years … but once he'd accepted that you were my choice he stood by you loyally, and when the worst happened he visited you in prison, the only member of my family to do so, and did what he could to see things right between us.

I am going to try to get hold of another copy for the Blackers, because they also have nothing but admiraton for you as an artist. I wish you had inscribed it for me, for old time's sake … "To Constance, from Oscar" … I once had an inscribed copy of everything you'd ever written, but the bailiffs took most of them when they ransacked our house - did you know that, Oscar?

I shall show this to the Ranee when I see her later this afternoon. Oh Oscar, to read it in its entirely has made me cry again! I cannot bear it, I cannot bear to think of you in prison, and of all the wounds inflicted there upon your tender heart. I do not think I will ever get over the shock of that first visit to you at Wandsworth, when I could neither see you properly nor touch you at all, nor say anything to help you in your degradation and pain. That two souls who had loved one another so much should have had to meet under such conditions! That "a poet and a poem", as you once described us, should be forced to converse through those hideous bars!

Hotel Bristol
Monaco
21st of February 1898

Well Oscar, by now I imagine that you will have received my letter agreeing to restore your allowance. I was greatly touched by what you wrote to me, and it was good to hear from you directly, instead of the usual complaining messages delivered via Robbie. I know that he is doing his best in a difficult position, but I would much prefer to have you communicate with me yourself. I need not tell you how pleased I am to hear that you have left A.D. You do not tell me the circumstances, but I hear from other sources that you have accepted £200 from Lady Q. on the condition that you do not see her son again. It all sounds rather sordid, and I suppose you would tell me that I have helped to make it so, as you did upon that other occasion. Oh Oscar, that letter really was the letter of a madman, and I have destroyed it so that I will never have to read it again.

  You see how the subject of money brings out the worst in me! It makes me sound so spiteful and ungenerous, but I do not mean to be ungenerous Oscar, in fact I am going to prepare a codicil to my will so that if I die before you, your allowance from the settlement will continue. The rest will be for our children, of course.

I wish you would let me pay your hotel bill direct. No wonder the money seems insufficient if you squander it as I know you do. I paid just four marks a day at Heidelberg. But if you had more money you would spend it all, and do no work.

I am staying here in Monaco with Vivian. He has leave of absence from the Collegio, and shares my room here at the Hotel. Oh Oscar, he is so sweet and gentle and clever! You would be proud of him. The Jesuits are pleased with his progress, and his health improves in the climate here. He reminds me very much of you - he has your eyes, deep set and full of dreams. He has your mouth too – Cyril's is more finely shaped, like my own. Every time I look at Vivian, I see the little boy you must once have been, and it breaks my heart. I think that is why I have not been able to tell him (as yet he has not asked) about what happened to you. Cyril is all honour and discretion, and will have kept his promise not to say anything, I think – though now and again I do wonder – but surely Vivian would have said something to me, if he knew or suspected that you've been in prison?

I see in our son's eyes the innocence, the hope you must once have had, and I just cannot bring myself to shatter it now. Oh, may God protect him from all that has cursed you!

My greatest fear however – you will think it foolish, but one has to consider these things – is that if I should die while he is still young, he may hear it from someone else, and in a way that will bring far greater pain. That is why I had resolved to tell him, but these precious days are going so fast, and my heart shrinks from the task. Would it be too cowardly to write him a letter when I return to Nervi? But then he would have to bear it all alone, with me far away ... oh, I don't know what to do. He tells me that he treasures my letters and reads them again and again, and I have promised to write him a long one before I go to Genoa – the prospect of my operation frightens him, and I wish now that I had not told him about it. I try to make light of it. What can one do with so sensitive a child? Oh Oscar, I just can't add to his burden of anxiety at such a time. It will have to wait.

One thing bothers me much, Oscar. Do you think that when the children were little we favoured Cyril too obviously? I'm afraid that we did ... I have noticed a tendency in Vivian to give way too easily, to take the part of the underdog, and I believe this to be our fault. I could not combat your disappointment over his not being the daughter you hoped for, and to this was soon added a disappointment of my own – we were obviously not going to have any more children, and I knew that it was my time of carrying Vivian that had been the last straw for you. It was not that I was desperate for more children, but you never really came back to me after Vivian was born, and I'm afraid that I blamed him, innocent baby that he was ... and then finally you came to me with that feeble, cowardly excuse. How little respect you must have had for me, to try to palm me off with a story like that! And how you underestimated me then! I despised you for your relief when I pretended to accept it. For the first time in our marriage, I truly depised you.

1st of May 1887
One o'clock a.m.

I cannot go to sleep tonight, and feel as though I never will again. My eyes are swollen so that I can hardly focus on the page before me, and yet I feel that to write something down is the only way to relieve myself of this terrible anger and pain. Oscar is still out – I suppose he imagines that I will be safely asleep by the time he returns from wherever it is he has gone to. Well, it will do him no harm to see a light burning in my room and to know that I, too, am wakeful.

He came to me this evening after dinner, when we had said good night to the children – he followed me from the nursery into my room here. He hummed and hawed, and shifted from foot to foot, and eventually brought up a conversation we'd had a few days ago when I chaffed him to the effect that he did not find me attractive now that I was the mother of two children. I freely admit that the laughter was somewhat hollow, and that I'd intended him to feel the barbs beneath the chaffing. The incident had obviously given him pause for thought, for now he announced to me, in serious tones and with fear in his eyes, that he had something to tell me of which he was deeply ashamed, and which he had wished to conceal from me but must now explain, clearly and honestly, as it would affect both our lives. He added that he had been urged to take this step by a medical practitioner – he told me the name, but in my alarm I failed to register it – I know it was not a name I'd ever heard before. I am not quite sure what I thought he was going to say – my mind was all unfocussed, I just wanted him to come out with it, to get it over – but I thought that whatever it was, it would at least be the truth!

He than announced that we can never resume normal relations as man and wife. The reason he has given is a resurgence of a certain condition, contracted from a liaison of the usual sordid and mercenary kind during his student days at Oxford.

It sounds plausible, I know. That he visited such women I do not doubt, for I know from Otho that this is regarded almost as part of the curriculum at both our noble seats of learning. Also he admitted something of the sort to me before we were married. But he never mentioned such consequences even during our most intimate talks (and we had sworn to tell one another everything – I told him everything!) - and to speak of it now, after months of excuses – all my instincts tell me that it is another excuse, but a final one. It is something that I cannot question, and certainly cannot discuss with anyone else. If I say outright that I do not believe him, he has only to stand his ground. And what do I want him to say? Do I really want to hear the truth?

"I am sorry, my dear, I am still very fond of you but I feel no desire for you any more; in fact, if you must know, your body has become disgusting to me, and I have had to force myself to play the part of a husband to you over these past few months." Could I bear to hear him say that?

And I, could I bear to tell my truth - "I still want you, Oscar, and desire you as much as ever; I shall miss your passion, your mastery and shyness, your strength and sweetness." No! I shall never say it. I half regret having written it. I will never humiliate myself, never ask him, never show him by look, word or deed that I feel anything other than equanimity, maybe even relief, at the way our lives must be from now on.

I believe that I carried it off quite well. I remained calm, though he could see I was shocked. I was not reproachful, and I thanked him – fellow hypocrite that I am! - for his honesty, his thoughtfulness. I let him think that I believed him. I told him one truth, that I still loved him. I let him go.

(And where will he go? That is what I want to know, that is what I <u>will</u> know in time, I swear it. I do not believe for a moment that he will compound the fiction by remaining celibate. If he had stayed at home, I might have given him the benefit of the doubt – but he is not at home. He has gone out this very evening. Where does he go, and with whom? Whom does he favour over me?   Who is the recipient of those kisses, those sighs, that urgency of breath? It is too painful to contemplate. But we shall see. We shall see. And then, God help me, and God help him.)

And I, where shall I go? But of course, there is no door open for me. I shall have to cultivate a dignified celibacy, as other scorned wives do – others, whom I used to pity! But I shall do it, since I have no choice. I shall tend the shrine of my home, I shall nurture my babies, I shall move like a queen amongst my gold and ivory. And I shall do more. I shall take up my pen again, I shall pursue my own interests, I shall – I shall do something, I swear it. Others will remind him constantly, when they speak of me, that I am a woman of some importance in my own right.

He has returned. He has gone up to his room. I heard him pause before my door, and then retreat. He knows, then, that my light is burning, that I am wakeful. Let him wonder. I feel a bird with talons awakening within me. I feel a soul within me as great as his.

It is May Day already. In the morning, I shall wear green.

Would you have been surprised, Oscar, to read all this? I wonder. But you will certainly be surprised to hear that it is all lies. Why did I write down such lies?

That is not to say that I believed you after all; I was not lying about that, but about my own inner feelings. I did not want your desire any more,

Oscar. Not since I was expecting Cyril, if truth be told. And that was not because I felt myself to be in any way disgusting, or if I did it was only the feeling of the moment; it was because I felt myself to be too sacred. It was *I* who should have proclaimed the taboo – it was not your place to reject *me*. I should have been sole possessor of my body, to give or to withhold, but you cheated me of this. You pre-empted me, on that occasion, and made it your prerogative to withdraw so that I became the recipient of your compassion instead of your respectful obedience. Is it any wonder that I could not admit such things even to myself? I was disarmed, and left with a tongueless anger. Well, let it be recorded now, Oscar, that you gave me the freedom I would have chosen myself, but that I would gladly have flung it back in your face and redoubled my pretence of ardour, so great was my anger at having no choice in the matter.

This long detour has made me forget to mention a matter of great importance! Vivian has told me something very serious, which I suppose I ought to have foreseen: he wishes to convert, to go over to Rome, to 'become a Cat', as we used to say. What should I do? In principle I am not against it, and I would be a great hypocrite if I were, for of course I once contemplated taking that very step myself! You dissuaded me, didn't you, on the grounds that it would affect the boys' chances of going to Eton. Well, now that any such chance has well and truly evaporated – there is scope for irony here, and recrimination, but I will restrain myself - do you think I should respect our son's spiritual choice at such a young age? The trouble is that Adrian Hope will definitely be against it, and he is, for better or worse, Vivian's guardian, and I have to ask for his advice, and cannot officially seek yours. And where would we find a Catholic school in England for him, supposing we return? It would have to be Stonyhurst, I suppose...

Anyway, I have urged him to wait for a year or two – I know that at his age that seems a cruel length of time, but I am sure that his tutors, if they are wise, will understand. Perhaps I will ask the Princess to have a word. She always speaks kindly of you, by the way, Oscar; she has a finely tuned appreciation of your genius which has not been slackened by your misfortune. Indeed, the atmosphere here in Monaco is so relaxed, so liberal, that the general mood is one of amusement (if that can be called appropriate!) at the severity of our English laws. It is quite openly spoken of, that many English exiles are living on the Continent in order to escape just such rigours of justice as you have suffered. I cannot say that I feel much amusement at the situation, and I am sure that you do not either, but it's heartening to see that it is possible for civilised people to view these matters in a kinder light. Dare I say that it gives one hope for the future – not for your future of course, or mine, but for those who may come after us? Such senseless suffering, and the blighting of innocent lives (I mean our children's, of course) could be avoided …

1st of March 1898
Nervi

I am back at the Villa now, Oscar, as you see. I did not, in the end, say anything to Vivian - I feel such a coward, but as I said, he is already worrying about my operation and I just cannot pile any further burden upon him at this time. I am suffering, of course, from the return journey ... in fact I have been confined to bed ever since I arrived, with Maria fussing over me (what would I do without her? She is more than just a maid to me now – she has become a loyal and devoted companion). But I have not been idle – I have been making use of my enforced bed rest to make further inroads into these old diaries – I've read over two years' worth of entries in the last two days!

"I shall do *something*", I had written in May 1887, "I swear it!" And during those last few years of the last decade, I did so much ... I find myself amazed, not only at the energy I once had, but also at the conflicted emotions and passions I recorded as I threw myself one month into this activity and the next into that – searching desperately, I see with hindsight, for an independent identity, a safe harbour - any port, as they say, in a storm.

14th of July 1887

Am spending a quiet afternoon recovering from the rigours of yesterday. This morning we went for a walk with the children before it became too hot, and were recognised by many fellow strollers in the Park. We were complimented frequently on the boys' good looks and air of robust health, which made us both very proud. O. took my arm, and I flatter myself we made an extremely handsome and distinguished couple!

The Lady's Pictorial is going to do an article on yesterday's party, and I know that it will be favourably reported as it went very well. I am glad now that my mother came, if only so that she could see how successfully I manage my house and family, and how I have gained in confidence and social poise – something she used almost to discourage in me, I now realise. I hope that they took particular note of my dress, for green-and-gold suits me, and the medieval style made me feel rather like Maid Marion – maybe next time I will specify fancy dress! (O. would perhaps not be appropriately cast as Robin Hood, but he could be a Richard Coeur de Lion amongst his courtiers.)

Nurse brought in Cyril and Baby, and they were perfectly well behaved and charming. Mrs Bram Stoker confided to me that if all children were as delightful in adult company, they would be regarded as a hostess's greatest asset and never banished to the nursery, which I took as a great compliment. Lady W. was imposing in a velvet headdress – I am less intimidated by her "Speranza" presence now that I am a literary hostess in my own right! It was fascinating to watch her hold sway over a bevy of adoring young men – she mesmerises her victims like a Hydra.

The house looked perfect, thank Heaven, and I can see now how right it was to have only roses for decoration – something O. insisted upon – he has become almost superstitious about roses of late. They gave the whole interior the appearance of a summer bower, and the white blooms in the tall blue vases, which I arranged myself, were particularly admired. Of course the guest list was chosen almost entirely by O. with a view to soliciting contributions for *The Woman's World,* which has become quite a literary publication under his editorship these last three months! But it was encouraging to receive several compliments on my own articles - and I was able to mention that I've also been asked to review for *The Lady's Pictorial*, which makes it clear that I do not write only for O.

I sound remarkably content, do I not? I was becoming a halfway decent actress after all, it seems, playing the "Mrs Oscar" that everyone assumed me to be, tending the shrine of my house, hosting literary parties and writing fashion articles. I'm amazed at how thoroughly I seem to have convinced myself that such a life was not only bearable, but satisfying … more lies, of course, designed to pacify the restless agitation of my spirit. What I really needed, of course, was a Cause to immerse myself in - and I was about to get one!

21st October 1887

Something really extraordinary happened this morning. I received an unexpected visit from a lady I have met only once before, and that only briefly at Lady W.'s a few weeks ago, who after ten minutes' conversation seems to have persuaded me to become involved in a political organisation! It all seems rather unreal, and certainly rather unwise – I have not yet informed O. that I've agreed to attend a meeting of the Chelsea branch of the Women's Liberal Association …

Was that really all that I had to say about my first meeting with Margaret? I can picture the scene as clearly as if it were yesterday.

Sharp autumn sunlight gilded the rail of the balustrade as I descended the stairs to the library, where my unknown visitor was waiting. Assuming that she had come to visit you, not knowing that you were from home, and therefore that my reception of her would be a mere formality, I had not bothered to have her shown up to the drawing room.

As I entered the room she was standing with her back to the door, inspecting the contents of our bookshelves through a lorgnette. I coughed politely, and she turned. I saw a tall, imposing woman of between fifty and sixty years, her dark hair, in which a few streaks of grey were detectable, drawn back severely into a plain knot. Her face was heavy, the jawline almost masculine, but one's attention was immediately absorbed by her eyes, which were deep set and very dark. The piercing intensity of her gaze startled me, and I managed only a rather hesitant "Good morning" before she addressed me.

"Mrs Wilde – how good of you to see me. I see by your expression that you do not remember me, which is not surprising, since I was but one among many guests at your mother-in-law's gathering a couple of weeks ago. I believe we were introduced briefly – my name is Lady Margaret Sandhurst, and I had a most interesting conversation with your husband about Irish Home Rule. I gather Mr Wilde is not at home?"

"No, he has business to attend to this morning, but when he hears that you have called, Lady Sandhurst, I am sure he will -"

"Good. For it was you that I came to see, and I am glad of the opportunity to talk with you alone. Lady Wilde informs me that you take a favourable view of women's involvement in the political sphere?"

"I – yes, I do remember you, Lady Sandhurst, and I – I beg your pardon?"

She laughed. "I see that I have taken you by surprise, my dear! Do forgive me. It is my way, I always neglect the small talk and launch straight in. Sit down, Mrs Wilde, and let me introduce myself a little more fully."

She motioned me to one of my own chairs and

took the other herself. I sat obediently, too much at a loss to utter a word.

I *do* remember meeting her at your mother's, and I remember your saying to me afterwards that the introduction was a ploy to persuade you to print one of her stirring political lectures in *Womans World*, and that you were wondering whether such a bold step would prove successful with the readership. She seemed much more interested in you than in me, although she paid me the usual compliments – I actually remember thinking that she must find me dull and insipid, and chafing inwardly at my inability to conjure up any astute political comments. What she could possibly have to say to me privately I could not imagine; but I was about to find out.

"Well, my dear, I don't know whether Lady Wilde will have told you, but my husband died some years ago leaving our eldest son to inherit the title and all the cares and concerns that go with it, and leaving me a Dowager with ample means and time on my hands to boot. So I have been fortunate enough to be able to devote my life, from that time onwards, to one of the greatest issues of modern times – female emancipaton in the political sphere. I am the President of the Marylebone branch of an organisation you may perhaps have heard of – the Women's Liberal Association."

"I have heard Lady Wilde mention it, always with great approbation."

"Ah! Dear Speranza! We are yokefellows in the cause, she and I, but my approach is a little less literary than hers, a little more *practical*. Now she tells me that you and your husband are both of the Liberal persuasion, and that you yourself have often expressed concern over the social ills which blight our so-called enlightened times – you have more than once given your support at charitable bazaars, for instance, for the relief of the East End poor."

"Yes, that is true, and I am ashamed of doing so little. But Oscar -"

"And you have expressed yourself quite strongly, I believe, on the subject of the heavy burden borne by working women; the endless drudgery and continual childbearing, so injurious to health and dignity alike, and the constant fear of abuse at the hands of their men."

"Yes, yes, it is a state of affairs which I find appalling, and one has only to look out of the back windows of this house, Lady Sandhurst, which overlook the Paradise Row slums, to see -"

"Excellent. You are also, I gather, a member of the Rational Dress Society, and therefore no stranger to the task of calling for reform. You realise that the only way to effect change is to take political action? To lobby Government for changes in legislation?"

"Well, I can see that all our charitable efforts are woefully inadequate; but I don't really see that the cause of rational dress -"

"Mrs Wilde, you are just the woman I am looking for! You see, we are in urgent need of new members – preferably influential ones – and you are ideal. Can I persuade you to come along to the next meeting of our Chelsea branch? I will be speaking myself; it will be an excellent opportunity for you to meet the other members and to gain a clearer picture of the Association's aims and objectives. Do come – I'm sure you will find it enjoyable and stimulating, if nothing else."

"Well – I will come along to a meeting with pleasure, Lady Sandhurst, but really I do think you overestimate the amount that I could contribute to a political movement. I have no political experience at all, whatever Lady Wilde may say – the Rational Dress Society may value my knowledge of the history of fashion, but I can hardly count that as political! Nor has my charitable work afforded me a very clear picture of the social structures behind the conditions which concern all right-minded people – my involvement has been purely subjective, and I'm afraid you will find me very ill-informed. Besides, I have no – no courage, no ability for public speaking and that sort of thing ..."

"Nonsense, my dear Mrs Wilde! You have the one quality that is necessary – the ability to see that something is wrong. You would be surprised how many people are quite blind to that simple fact – often deliberately so, I'm afraid. And you are quite wrong about the political implications of women's dress – they are very clear indeed, to me at least. As for courage, as for information, well both can be acquired very easily – wait and see! And in any case, there is something you can do right away, which I think you will find more in your usual line, and which will be of invaluable help to me – I have a house for incurables, in the Marylebone Road – many of them are children, and I know that as a mother the plight of children must be dear to your heart. We are in urgent need of help, especially financial help – perhaps you could organise a bazaar, or something of that sort? If you would like to visit first, that can easily be arranged. Do think about it. Look, I will write down for you the time, date and place of the W.L.A. Meeting. If you can come, I will see you there, and we can discuss things further when you've had a little time to get your thoughts in order. Will that suit you? There."

She handed me a torn scrap of paper on which she had hastily scribbled the information. I looked at it bemusedly.

"Yes ..." I said slowly, "I will try to come, Lady Sandhurst. I should like to. I will have to have a word with my husband, of course."

"Of course, by all means – but do not let your husband stand in your way, Mrs Wilde. I never did. Women will never have a say in the running of our country while they let their husbands dictate to them in every sphere of life. Well, goodbye my dear – no, please don't bother to ring, I can see myself out. I look forward to seeing you next week!"

I rose in her wake, and followed her to the door. When she had gone, I returned to the library and tried to make sense of it all.

I was already under her spell. There was a magnetic force to her personality which I could not help but compare to the fascination exerted by your mother – but it was like placing a bouquet of living flowers next to a magnificent dried arrangement.

21st of December 1887

Have just returned from Marylebone, where Margaret has made a wonderful job of creating a Christmas atmosphere – it will be the first real Christmas that some of those poor little mites have ever seen. There is to be goose for all who are well enough to eat it, and all the trimmings too!

I find that it distresses me less now to witness the plight of those poor children – not because I am becoming hardened to poverty and suffering, or in any way accepting of the appalling conditions in which so many of our fellow Englishmen and women are forced to live, but because I have become less dainty, less fragile, less concerned to preserve the illusion that just because I am comfortable in this life, all is as it should be. I know that I have Margaret to thank for that. After my first visit I swore that I would never go again, but now I am keener than ever to do what I can, and Margaret has proposed that I use my connections to organise a bazaar for the New Year – one often finds people that little bit more generous just after Christmas – which will hopefully raise a good sum of money, so badly needed just now.

There is one little boy there who is, Margaret assures me, the same age as Cyril, though he is so much smaller – and his limbs are all twisted, and he lay on his bed gazing up at me with such huge, sorrowful eyes – it was all I could do to hold back the tears. I hope and pray with all my heart that

Margaret may effect one of her miraculous cures upon him ... in the meantime, I have promised to bring along my copy of *The Bairns' Annual* and to read aloud from it. I feel a little shy of reading my own work, but Margaret insists that "Was It A Dream?" is exactly the kind of story that will enthrall and entertain the children, and make them forget their suffering for a while, poor little things. I feel privileged to think that my first published story, short and insignificant though it is, may bring happiness to the children of the poor as well as to those of the rich, at Christmas time.

Yes, I made a good start, not least as regards my literary career – it was one of our own Japanese fans that gave me the idea of bringing the Stork pictured upon it to life, and granting him his wish to see his homeland once again! I lied, though, about becoming less dainty and fragile. It never ceased to distress me, to see the plight of poor innocent children born into poverty, unemployment and disease. It never ceased to tug at my conscience, to look out of our back windows and see the slums of Paradise Row, the children running barefoot in the street, the women pegging out dirty clothing washed in dirty water, the drunken, loutish men weaving their way home along the back alleyway. It was a world so alien, and so repugnant to me, that I had to steel my soul to immerse even the tip of my toe into it. And the tip of my toe is all that I ever did immerse, I am ashamed to say – within less than a year I was back on more comfortable ground, having taken over the editorship of the Rational

Dress Society's *Gazette*. You expressed your relief in no uncertain terms, I remember; I kept mine to myself.

11th of September 1888

Today I received my invitation, officially in writing, to lecture for the Rational Dress Society at the Somerville Club! Although I had been forewarned, it was still exciting to open and read it. I keep having to remind myself that it will not be the first time I have spoken in public, but it will be the first time I have taken on a wider audience at a well-publicised event! The Press will almost certainly be there, and as editor of the Society's *Gazette* I must make a good impression.

The date is to be 6th of November, so I have plenty of time to prepare. I must keep myself free of course for Vyvyan's birthday - he is to have a party with red paper dragons ... fortunately my leg has been less painful recently, so I will not be dragging myself around as I have been these last few months. No-one seems to know the cause of my lameness but I'm so glad it has proved to be temporary, for I can hardly follow the doctor's instructions to rest with so much going on!

Our next meeting is at Lady Harberton's so we will discuss our strategy there. But I know that attendance is to be for ladies only, which is a great relief, and that the subject matter should be general, as we hope to win over many who might not automatically be familiar with the Society's aims and objectives. This should be a good opportunity to dispel the myth that rational dress is in any way unfeminine or immodest, as our critics are so fond of alleging ...

I have already thought of a title – "Clothed In Our Right Minds". The quotation from St Paul should dispel any aura of frivolity or eccentricity still clinging to the subject in people's minds. I will prepare a rough outline before the meeting at Lady H's, and then work on it further subject to the others' approval. I am particularly anxious to impress Mrs Stopes, who will be our hostess for the December meeting, because I have heard that she is thinking of asking me to speak on that occasion and this may enhance her opinion of me, and decide her!

Of course I cannot wait to tell Margaret. I know she will be pleased, for she has always encouraged me, even though she knew that editing the Gazette would prevent me from helping in her work as much as I used to ... but she says it is important that I branch out and make use of my own area of expertise (such as it is! I never imagined that my interest in fashion would lead me into such deep waters!) I have not yet broadcast the news to Lady W. - I know she will want to be present, and I do hope she will not be too insistent on my making frequent allustion to the "Literary Dress", and how swathing oneself in Greek drapery encourages an identification with this or that goddess, and what not. I really do want us to be taken seriously on this occasion!

I showed the invitation to O. at breakfast, and he seemed quite pleased – his support means much to me, of course, though it irks me considerably to hear that some believe me to be using the Society as a vehicle for <u>his</u> ideas on dress. I am sometimes tempted to make public his private opinion of the divided skirt – so very un-Attic! - and he <u>will</u> keep trying to dress the boys up as Little Lord Fauntleroy, which is hardly consistent with our espousal of non-restrictive clothing for children ...

A little snipe at you there, I see, Oscar. It must have been increasingly obvious that I was chafing under your yoke – I was quite waspish and cantankerous at home, as I remember. Were you casting around, I wonder, for a solution to our disharmony before you came up with the simple idea of changing the yoke?

12th of November 1888

Oh, I am in such a state of nerves about tomorrow! I am half inclined to back out, but O. would be so angry if I did. He encouraged my interest in Theosophy from the start, of course, both he and Speranza being great admirers of Mme Blavatsky; and I found her ideas and her teaching inspirational, and would have stayed quite happy if only we could have stuck with her. I never in my wildest dreams imagined that my fascination for the esoteric would take me this far ... oh, why did I ever agree to meet Mr Mathers?

<u>That</u> was O.'s idea also, of course. He finds the concept of a "Hermetic Order of the Golden Dawn" irresistible, he likes to roll the words off his tongue and smack his lips over them. But he does not wish to risk his growing reputation by publicly allying himself with such a radical nonconformity, so he has persuaded <u>me</u> to undergo the initiation, and fool that I am I have gone along with it; and tomorrow is the day, and I am absolutely terrified.

To cap it all, I must not reveal the details of the ceremony, or any of the hidden teaching I will then be eligible to receive, to a living soul; I am even forbidden to write about it in my diary, on pain of I don't know what. O. seems to think that this oath will not apply to conversations with him, "there being no secrets between husband and wife" – an irony coming from him, if ever there was one! He has plenty of secrets from <u>me</u>, I hardly know where he is half the time! And the worst of it is, I know exactly why he has engineered me into this position – he is planning to write a story about the supernatural, and he wants material.

I should have stood up to him, I should have told him to do his own underhand research, and leave me out of it. But Mr Mathers is so persuasive, as is the Comtesse de Brémont who is to be initiated with me, and now I have agreed to go along with it and it's too late to back out. I wonder what

dreadful oath I will have to take? Whether I will
have the courage to break it, and write about it in
this diary? I have already chosen my personal
motto – that is, I chose it from those on offer – it is
to be Qui Patitur Vincit, "He Who Endures,
Conquers". By this time tomorrow I will have
endured the initial ceremony, at least. I only hope I
can get through it without fainting ...

And that, believe it or not, is it! That is all I can
find, throughout the whole diary – well, as far as
I've been able to skim forward – about my
involvement with the Hermetic Order of the Golden
Dawn, apart from a brief mention of my intention to
allow my membership to lapse. I kept my promise,
then, not to record or impart any esoteric matters, at
least as regards the diary - a promise made, Oscar,
under pain of being *"slain or paralysed without
visible weapon as if blasted by the lightning flash"*,
as I dutifully revealed to you, still trembling
uncontrollably in the aftermath. Oh, that dreadful
ceremony ... the black tunic, the blindfold, the cord
wound about my waist ... you said it was all
borrowed from the Masons, that it was mere
theatrics, and you *laughed* at me, Oscar, for taking
it so seriously. And you persuaded me to continue,
to progress from the Neophyte Grade through all the
others, and attend all those bizarre rituals made up
by Samuel Mathers, and do all that homework –
well, you supervised me in that, of course, and
together we made a superficial study of the Hebrew
language, the Kabbalah, the rudiments of Astrology

and the symbolism of the Tarot - it was not that I had insufficient intelligence or application for such study, but rather that you wanted to inform yourself vicariously. But be that as it may, I did all that in secret, along with my political work, along with preparing my own little book, along with running my home - and the result was that I neglected my children. I left them to Nurse to manage, I had them packed off to the family in Dublin – and Vyvyan still a baby – and I was not the kind, attentive mother I had sworn to be. And now, Oscar, I weep to think of the precious moments missed, and all the little achievements that went unpraised and the little upsets and tumbles unkissed, and I cannot forgive myself, or you.

And Oscar, just think. Think about what has happened to us both. The creeping paralysis for me, the lightning blast for you. It frightens me, that whole episode frightens me now almost as much as it did then. Is it any wonder that almost as soon as I left the Order I took refuge in the arms of the Church?

But you got what you wanted out of it, didn't you Oscar – a background against which to paint *The Picture of Dorian Gray.*

10th of January 1889

Have just returned from visiting Margaret. We are both so excited about the elections – only one week to go now. Margaret does not appear at all nervous, unlike myself – but I do feel confident that all our hard campaigning will bear fruit. Everyone is predicting that the Progressive candidate is bound to win, and the fact that she is a woman actually seems to be working in our favour! To have three women standing for the London County Council, and one of them my dearest friend - it seems too magnificent to be true. Hoorah for the Local Government Act, which has made all this possible! Surely now we will begin to see a change in legislation, culminating – who knows how soon? - in female enfranchisement, a logical and basic right for every educated woman that can surely not be witheld for much longer.

Tomorrow will see the last meeting of the Chelsea Committee before the event. Margaret wants me to open the proceedings, though surely the honour should go to her ... we are all behind her, heart and soul ...

Oh, this is hard to read. Poor, dear Margaret! How full of optimism we were, how trusting, how confident – and how blissfully unaware of the travails to come ...

21st of March 1889

This morning I received a very amusing letter from Carrie Blacker, who writes to congratulate me on the publication of "There Was Once". She says that their copy will stand side by side with "The Happy Prince" on their bookshelf as proof that they know at least one family who believe in fairies!

It is kind of her to pretend to compare my work with O.'s, when he made up all those stories out of his own head – albeit with a few suggestions from me – whereas I have been content merely to reproduce tried and tested favourites; but I must confess that it was thrilling to be able to hold my own little volume in my hand – the subtitle is "Grandma's Stories, retold by Mrs Oscar Wilde" – a tribute, of course, to dear Mama Mary, whose vivid storytelling first inspired me to explore the world of my imagination. Mr Lawson's illustrations have come out beautifully, and the finished effect is most attractive.

O. is very pleased about the book, for it reflects well on him to have a literary wife, and to see his name, prefaced by "Mrs", on yet another front cover. He is working, by the way, on a new story which he says will be different from anything he has written so far, about Shakespeare's Sonnets. He says he can produce no small evidence that they were addressed not to a woman, as is commonly supposed, but to another man! I told him that even if this is true, he would be mad to say so directly; but he insists that he will approach the matter obliquely, so that it will not give offence. He is much engrossed in it, and does not read it to me as he did the fairy stories. It all seems rather cloak-and-dagger …

Carrie also writes, "I hear you and Lady Sandhurst have been turning the world upside down! How magnificent!"

Well, that is a kind exaggeration, for the Brixton Division of the London County Council is hardly "the world", especially when viewed from Paris! But her support is encouraging, particularly so at the moment; she obviously has not heard that Margaret's election has been challenged. We are appealing, of course; surely no court is going to uphold the deselection of an elected Councillor, especially one with so large a majority, purely on the grounds of her sex? It says much about the petty and spiteful nature of Mr Beresford Hope that he can bring such a ridiculous case against an opponent who has beaten him fairly and squarely. Apparently he is relying solely upon the fact that the Act is couched in masculine terms, which of course is true of all legal language, and ecclesiastical language too. But no-one takes it literally - that would be ridiculous! When one speaks, for example, of "the brotherhood of man", or "the rights of man", one is not excluding the female sex! Surely we cannot lose our victory on such a technicality? It is enough to make one despair, although Margaret forges ahead as gallantly as ever.

Well, we know how that turned out, don't we Oscar? In the June, we were finally forced to concede defeat – Margaret's appeal failed, and her seat was lost. My entry for that fateful day simply reads as follows, all in capitals:

DAY OF MIS-JUDGEMENT. I HAVE COMPLETELY
LOST FAITH IN THE JUSTICE AND IMPARTIALITY OF
THE ENGLISH LEGAL SYSTEM.

It is a sentiment I should have taken more securely
to heart, is it not?

Anyway, the disillusionment took a toll on all of us
– all of the ladies, I mean. If a woman could not
win a seat on the London County Council, what
hope was there for the franchise? Margaret became
disheartened, and I became ill – mainly due to
nerves, of course - I could not sleep, I became
irritable and querulous, and of course you never
could bear that so I spent the summer with the
Thursfields in Yorkshire in search of rest and
recuperation. And my relationship with Margaret
suffered also – I had put her on so high a pedestal,
and her disillusionment became mine also, so that I
no longer had my safe harbour, but must go out in
the storm to look for another. It was cruel and
ungrateful of me, I freely admit; but I was already
coming under the influence of a quieter, less
strident role model; though one no less brave, both
spiritually and politically ...

21st of September 1889
Babbacombe Cliff

I am writing this in the most charming surroundings,
at Lady Mount-Temple's home in Torquay. It was so
kind of her to invite me and the boys while O. is

away and I think this is going to be exactly the tonic I need after all my political exertion and consequent illness and fatigue.

They have a tower here called the Crow's Nest which the boys delight in, and an abundance of Burne-Jones stained glass, and Morris wallpaper ... each room is named after its featured design: Rose, Marigold, Lily, etc. But the most magical room is "Wonderland", at the heart of the house, beautifully decorated with scenes from Lewis Carroll's story. This place really does feel like a Wonderland to me, after the dirt and the grime and the drudge of London.

Lady M-T is so kind. She has been a widow for over a year now, and I think she values the company. In spite of having been almost neighbours in London, we have only just graduated to first-name terms and I'm still a little in awe of her, with her dignified, old-fashioned bearing, and snow-white hair. She does not have Margaret's galvanising energy, but rather a spiritual quality about her that is almost mesmeric. I feel myself quieten at the sound of her voice, I feel my limbs grow heavy, I feel at peace.

Georgina is of the High Church persuasion, and takes the Sacrament almost daily – that is why, no doubt, she carries such a numinous presence. It humbles me, and puts the theatrical antics of the G.D. into a most unflattering perspective. I feared at first that she would not approve of my interest in Theosophy and Hermeticism, but she is obviously of no narrow creed – Mr Frederic Myers of the Society for Psychical Research is apparently a frequent visitor here! I have not told her about my involvement with the G.D. There is no need, as I am determined now to let my membership lapse.

 Oh, it is so wonderful to be here, in this calm and beautiful place, after all the agitation of the past months. I finally feel safe, anchored, at home.

 O. of course is <u>not</u> at home. To be honest, I am not sure exactly where he is ...

And so began the second great friendship of my life. Dear Georgina was to become my rock, a true Mother to me in all my subsequent troubles. She was a good friend to you too, Oscar, was she not? But you never realised, I suspect, the extent to which I confided in her, or how many times she persuaded me, in the later years, to pull our marriage back from the brink. She encouraged me, too, to persevere in my political and literary endeavours, and buoyed up by her faith in me I really did begin to rise once more on my wings ... how long would they have borne me up, I wonder, how high might I have soared, had "Apollo" not strayed across my path with his burning chariot to reduce them to feathers and wax?

And that, Oscar, more or less concludes my two days' retrospective indulgence, my reacquaintance with my younger self and all that I achieved in those heady years. It all feels like a lifetime ago. I think of those years as a period of lost innocence, of happy ignorance and fond illusions. For while I was busy "branching out" and "discovering myself", you were well embarked upon your own journey of self-discovery, were you not? A journey that would lead you to the cliff's edge.

Villa Elvira
Nervi

6th of March 1898

A strange co-incidence – having mentioned a letter from Carrie Blacker in my last entry, I actually received one this morning. Apparently Carlos is on his way to Paris, and he has your address and strict instructions to visit you, which I am sure he will do. I hope you will not be offhand with him, Oscar; he has been a good friend to you, and also especially good to the boys over these last two years. I consult him more readily than I do Adrian, on all matters concerning their welfare. Truly he is one of the kindest men I have ever met. I would not mind at all if the Catholic faith produced a similar effect in Vivian.

I sent a copy of your *Ballad* to the Blackers, and Carrie says that they both found it moving and impressive, and that Carlos has taken it with him so that he may have it inscribed by the author! Is that not a tribute from a friend who truly appreciates you?

Carrie proposes that we spend the summer together, with the boys of course, and I am already looking forward to it. I do hope that my health will have improved by then; I am out of bed now but still housebound, and typewriting is virtually the only exercise I am allowed. Even my fingers feel weak and clumsy, hence the mistakes. But I do keep myself occupied, Oscar, besides writing this – what shall I call it? Epistle? Testament? Diary? It is all of these, and yet none of them - besides, as I say, all this delving into the past, I have taken up photography again! This I know will make you smile, for you chaffed me for taking my Kodak to Florence and returning with all those rolls of film whilst remaining thoroughly intimidated by the camera whenever I was obliged to pose. Unlike you, I was never confident in front of the lens, and the results were invariably mortifying... however the feeling is quite different at the other end of the lens, as I am rediscovering! The difficulty lies in finding enough willing victims. I do have a pleasant circle of friends here, mostly fellow expatriates introduced to me by the Ranee, and they oblige me from time to time, but more and more I find that I am turning to the natural world for inspiration – and now that Spring is well under way, the countryside would afford no shortage of opportunities for me to improve my technique, if only I were well enough to get out! Ah, dear.

I wonder if you would like it here, Oscar? I often indulge in daydreams of a visit from you. You would find it too quiet, no doubt. Was it too quiet at Naples? Not to your taste nor to his, I presume. Had you planned to escape, to hide away together? And now it has all fallen through. I seem to have spent half my life trying to escape, in one way or another; the fairy tales, the parties .. my militant days, if you can call them that, afforded me the best escape of all.

I can see the garden from my window. There are white flowers already – always my favourites, and your choice of flowers for me. At first you used to say they reflected my purity, that I was slim and graceful as a Madonna lily. Later I cultivated them as symbols of decline, of mourning – white roses, suitable for a funeral wreath, white sleep-inducing poppies ... I was fond of narcissi also, until you met Narcissus.

I have been leafing through our wonderful visitors' book from Tite Street, your present to me when we first moved into our House Beautiful. Thank heaven I managed to save it from the bailiffs! Do you remember how you inscribed the first page for me?

I can write no stately proem
As a prelude to my lay;
From a poet to a poem -
This is all I say.

For if of these fallen petals
One to you seem fair,
Love will waft it till it settles
On your hair.

And when wind and winter harden
All the loveless land,
It will whisper of the garden,
You will understand.

There are whispers of the garden all around me,

Oscar. There are white petals in my hair. And it was a very bitter understanding that awaited me, in that hard and loveless land towards which we were both steering.

And now, let me test your memory, Oscar. Let me see whether I cannot conjure up your past for you better than you can for yourself. There are voices coming from the smoking room – yours, Robbie's, John Gray's and Lionel Johnson's. The scent of Alexandrian tobacco wafts out to the landing, where June sunlight slants down into the stairwell. I linger there, listening to the sound of tinkling glasses and masculine laughter.

"Oh no, Oscar, this is too much! How, after *Dorian* – it will be going from the sublime to the ridiculous. Besides, you cannot base a whole play on the unrequited lust of an Israelite princess, not in this day and age."

"Why ever not? The West End Threatre, my dear Lionel, thrives on unrequited lust. Look at any play you care to name, and you will find that lust is the very pivot upon which the action turns."

"Yes, but a Biblical theme -"

"Oh, lust is a very Biblical theme. And anyway, I intend to make her Persian. Poetic licence, my dear, the prerogative of genius. The Israelites had no appreciation of sin."

"No, they quite disapproved of it, I'm told -"

"Whereas the Persians toasted the delights of the flesh in sugared wine, offered in chalices of jade and silver by sloe-eyed boys with dusky skin and rose-leaf lips ..."

"Robbie, what utter drivel. What do you know of Persia?"

"As much as you, I dare say, Dorian. I was merely offering a humble tribute to the exquisite style and taste of our host here."

"A very poor imitation then, and please *don't* call me Dorian."

"Mr Gray then, if we must be formal..."

"Oh Oscar, really, can't you stop him?"

"Stop him? But why? He is charming with vine leaves in his hair. At least he had the foresight to arrive suitably arrayed in leafy clusters, whereas you two are both obliged to borrow from me!"

"Yes, you are obliging us to drink sherry at half past eleven in the morning!"

"It is gone noon, I assure you! Let us toast the glorious noon with more of this golden nectar. Lionel?"

"Oscar, how can I refuse you?"

"Never try. John?"

"It is just gone half past eleven. I looked at my watch not five minutes ago."

"I will not have to do with guests who consult their watches in my presence. But if you insist, let us look at mine – there, you see my dear - the bawdy hand of the dial is e'en now upon the prick of noon!"

"Oh, really, Oscar!"

"But it is the Bard! Shakespeare's words, not mine! And am I not right? You see how time flies when you are listening to me? And now, are you going to drink some more of my sherry?"

"Oh, very well."

"There's no need to be so ungracious about it, dear, just because I was right and you were wrong. Petulance does *sometimes* become you, but not today. Today, let all be sweetness and light. Robbie, my sweet goblin, what *have* you been doing this morning? How came you thus to anticipate us? Robert, it is too tiresome when you giggle like that instead of replying to my questions. How can I discuss the delicious wantonness of Salome when you sit there gurgling gently like an overflowing waste pipe? I shall be forced to conclude that you require the services of a plumber .. oh really, what a vulgar sense of humour. *Do* try and pull yourself together, dear, and let us converse on serious matters. What were we talking about?"

"Lust, Oscar."

"Oh, surely not!"

"Persia. The West End theatre. Sodom and Gomorrah ..."

"Ah, the Cities of the Plain! Yes, it was just such a cradle that rocked Salome ..."

"I really don't see why. Dorian, perhaps."

"An English decadent and a Persian princess?"

"There is a Persian princess in all of us, don't you think?"

"Oh Oscar, how perceptive of you! I've been trying to keep it a secret!"

"Not in *you*, Robbie. A Persian princess would have more dignity. She certainly would not sit huddled at one end of a divan smirking tipsily to herself at half past – whatever it is in the morning. And you have never answered my question – where have you been?"

"Nowhere! I arose from my downy couch and came straight here. It is the residue of the night before ..."

"Ah, never refer to the night before! That should be a golden rule amongst all who take pleasure seriously."

"Now you are just quoting Pater."

"I most certainly am not. What do you know of Pater? He would never say such a thing. It is all mine, I assure you."

"So you do not, after all, "have the courage of the opinions of others"?"

"Never mention James Whistler to me!"

"Ah, so you admit it! It was Whistler's joke!"

"I admit nothing. I merely refer to the fact that a rather tedious aphorism puts me in mind of a rather tedious person, whom I would wish to forget in such delightful company as that which graces my drawing-room at present."

Laughter. You are one step ahead of them, as always.

"So now, seriously, Oscar – you have delighted us all with your subtlety in two wonderful stories which no-one else would have the audacity to write, let alone publish – I mean *The Portrait of Mr W.H.* And our *Dorian* – and now you announce that you are going to fling aside the mask of *double entendre* to reveal – what? A wanton girl and a reluctant prophet? Don't you realise how you will have disappointed us all?"

"I have no doubt that it will be a great disappointment to the shallow-minded, to those concerned only with the particular and not with the delicious conglomeration of the universal."

"Meaning?"

"Meaning the sins of the flesh, dear boy! A veritable feast! The apples of Sodom and the apples of Eden can be served at the same banquet, surely? Or else we reduce *la belle décadence* to the level of some sordid little club – there is the rest of the human race to consider!"

"As to that, I really neither know nor care. That is an opinion on which we must part company, Oscar, I think."

"So soon? My poor John, you will find the world a hard, inhospitable place when they expel you from Eden -"

"You think I am going to change, you think I am going to compromise my nature? Because I can assure you, Oscar -"

"No, no, I am merely saying that an artist must take his material from the whole of human experience. Especially if he is to produce West End plays."

"Ah, there you have it. You compromise, in order to appeal to the vulgar masses."

"Certainly I wish my talents to have universal acknowledgement. Genius cannot thrive in a backwater, John."

"A backwater! You disappoint me, Oscar."

"What, because I refuse to leave my house, my family, my Art, and elope with you to some seedy little lair in Bayswater?"

"There's no need to refer to that. I take back any such proposal. You mean to have your cake, and eat it too!"

"Most certainly I do; I would consider it vulgar and unimaginative not to!"

"Oh! And do you consider us all to be vulgar, and unimaginative?"

"Of course he does not, John, stop trying to provoke him. You are determined to create a deliberate misunderstanding."

"Am I?"

"Yes, and don't adopt that peevish tone with me. Life is a rich tapestry, and Oscar is the richer for being blessed with children, and an understanding wife."

"Thank you, Robbie. Your vine leaves become you. I *do* consider myself blessed."

"But *is* Constance understanding? Is she not rather just docile, and ignorant?"

"Constance, docile? You would not say that if you knew her!"

There is an edge to your laughter. I never did like John Gray, for all his good looks.

"Oh, so she knows, does she, where you spend the nocturnal hours?"

"I would consider it demeaning both to my wife and to myself to discuss such matters. We have an excellent understanding. She pursues her interests, and I mine."

"Oh come on, Oscar. We have all read what you have to say about these "understanding marriages" in *Dorian*. You mean that she consoles herself with High Church socialism in the company of eccentric old women -"

"John."

"It is all right, Robbie dear. It takes more than a little petulance to upset me. I am not Basil Hallward, and he is no Dorian, as he so rightly says. Now let us forget these petty quarrels and speak of my plans for *Salome*. I can promise you, you will not be disappointed, whatever you may think of the subject matter. It is to be written in French ..."

"In French! Ah, so this is the outcome of your sojourn in Paris!"

"But of course! I defy any artist to remain long in that delightful city without stumbling across a wellspring of inspiration bubbling up from its very stones ... ah, it is the cradle of decadence. Salome was conceived in Paris, and thither I shall return to attend her birth."

"I thought you said she was rocked on the Cities of the Plain!"

"And so she shall be, Lionel dear. One generally rocks the baby *after* it is born – at least, that is my experience. Yes, I shall go back to Paris in the autumn."

This is news to me. I had hoped that your long absences were over for the year. The whole of February and March, and most of May – and you did not write very often.

I have not been to Paris since our honeymoon ...

I tread carefully on the stairs, past the half open door, on my way to the sanctuary of my room. The sunlight has moved; a shadow steals across the upper landing. Just before I retreat from earshot, I hear Lionel Johnson say: "By the way, Oscar, there is a young cousin of mine who would very much like to meet you. He is just up at Oxford from

Winchester, and he claims to have read *Dorian* nine times running! He'll be down in London for the summer ..."

29th of June 1891

Today I returned from my tryst with Georgina - we went back to Cheyne Walk after Church, to take tea and discuss a rather disappointing homily — to find O. ensconced in his library with Lionel Johnson and his young cousin, a youth of seventeen who is apparently besotted with *Dorian Gray*. When he realised I was home, he brought them up to the drawing room to meet me. L.J. was as affected and pompous as ever, but I found Lord Alfred Douglas quite charming. He is the youngest son of the Marquess of Queensberry, but shows no sign of having inherited his father's pugnacious character — in fact he assures us that he takes solely after his mother, whom he adores, and to whom he has promised to introduce me. I must confess I would like to meet Lady Queensberry - she was the talk of London when she took the initiative in divorcing her husband! She must have suffered terribly, poor lady. Anyway, her son does her credit — he is very beautiful, very much O.'s ideal type, one can see that immediately. But he has none of the affected mannerisms which seem to be *de rigueur* amongst his other young men (always excepting Robbie); in fact, he has a sweet shyness about him which makes me feel quite maternal. He seemed overawed by O. (who was of course on top form), and spent a lot of time gazing at him adoringly. He says he has read Dorian fourteen times. He looks very Dorian-like himself, more so in fact than John Gray – although whereas I'm quite prepared to believe that <u>he</u> has a hideous portrait of himself hidden in the attic, one cannot think it of Lord Alfred. I do hope we will see more of him. He was very attentive to me, and complimented me on everything from the china to *Grandma's Stories*, of which his mother apparently has a copy. The children came in briefly, and he played peekaboo with Cyril and reduced the little fellow to such a paroxysm of laughter that I feared hysterics, and asked Nurse to take him out – but not before he had clambered onto Lord A.'s lap and kissed him soundly on the cheek, all of which the young man took with a very good grace.

The colour of his hair, by the way, is true gold, not the washed-out blond that so often passes under that description, and his eyes are a quite disturbing shade of blue – one could imagine him becoming either a saint, or a fanatic.

All in all, an unexpectedly pleasant afternoon. If all of O.'s friends were as nice, I would feel much happier about his spending so much time with them.

Well Oscar, if you ever read this, I hope it may make you feel as ashamed as it makes me feel humiliated. What a little fool I was - though not entirely oblivious, I realise, to his "fanatical" qualities. But who could have guessed, who would ever have suspected on first acquaintance, what poison lay beneath that sugar coating?

Yes, he was charming, and beautiful too, and I fell under his spell just as you did. That delightful impression of shyness, that artless adoration, those covert looks and lowered lashes must have been well rehearsed, as must all his attentiveness to me. What angers me particularly is that it took me so long, so pathetically long, to learn how low an opinion that boy held of my sex – unlike dear Robbie, but very like John Gray, and very like his own objectionable cousin, both of whom I had seen through immediately. "My first impressions of people are never wrong!" - was it really I who once said that? I remember that you looked at me curiously, and that I felt very clever.

"I soar above the miasma of the commonplace" - those words of course are your mother's, who allowed your father's mistress to come, veiled and silent, into the room where he lay dying, and to keep vigil there. "It was not because she did not love him," you explained to me, "but because she loved him very much, and he died with his heart full of gratitude towards her".

That was what I aspired to, that was how I fondly imagined myself – selfless, magnanimous, on a higher plane – and you, of course, like your father, would understand, and be full of gratitude. (Yes, I did sometimes picture you on your deathbed, Oscar, and myself allowing your friends, grieving and pale, to climb the stairs to your room and sit beside you;

quite a pleasurable anticipation, if truth be told!)

What did I know, exactly? Why is it so difficult to remember, burdened as I now am with too much knowledge? I had come to realise, obviously, that you preferred young men to women. The realisation never evoked disgust – on the contrary, it confirmed something I seemed to have always known about you. I do not think – I must be clear about this, if I can – that I ever imagined you engaged in sexual intimacy with them, not even with the golden boy, before Worthing. Therefore I did not feel betrayed, as I would have done had you taken a mistress. My position as your wife seemed secure enough, in spite of my enforced celibacy. I imagined you in romantic settings – among the dreaming spires, in candle-lit rooms, outside French cafés – laughing, flirting, brushing fingers perhaps, even embracing and kissing – nothing more than that. I found the picture charming. How little I sought to question myself! And yet I knew, in general if not in particular, to what offences Section Eleven of the Criminal Law Amendment Act referred; I knew that expressions of passionate affection between men could lead to something that was punishable by imprisonment with hard labour. The Cleveland Street scandal had been in all the papers a mere two years before; I'd read the reports and understood full well what sort of "immoral earnings" those telegraph boys were living on, and why Lord Arthur Somerset had to flee the country. Therefore, surely, I *must* have known that you were courting danger.

Perhaps I enjoyed a certain sense of power – the

knowledge that I could, if I wished, denounce you. Perhaps I insured myself with the knowledge that if you ever betrayed me utterly, I could betray you in return. There were many divorces, no shortage of scandals to furnish me with examples – my own brother Otho, the Queensberry affair, your poor brother Willie's disastrous marriage to his American wife - but so utterly had I convinced myself that I soared above the miasma of the commonplace that I have no clear recollection of thoughts like these. I suppose I never suspected that you would run the risk of arousing my outright hostility. And when it came to it, I did not even betray you properly; just half-heartedly, weakly, stupidly, because I could not summon the self-control to do otherwise.

That was also the summer of *A House Of Pomegranates* - do you remember? - which you dedicated to me. At least, the book as a whole was dedicated to me – each individual story was an offering to one of your friends. You compared it to a Cathedral, named for Our Lady but with side-chapels dedicated to various saints. It was a description I was happy to accept, indeed to rejoice in – I said as much to Georgina, knowing how she would appreciate the analogy. I even borrowed it to tell her that *my* Cathedral, dedicated to you, had a Lady Chapel where a lamp burned day and night for her, my "spiritual Mother".

Those were your last fairy tales, *our* last fairy tales, the end, finally, of our shared life; I can see that now. How I loved those stories! I loved their rich colours and archaic language. First came the young King and his little blue-eyed page, then the little Infanta and the loathsome dwarf – *"For the future, let those who come to play with me have no hearts"* – then the Star-Child who brought upon himself the curse of ugliness. How obsessed you were with beauty and ugliness! You hovered between Beauty as Truth and Beauty as Temptation, even as you abased yourself before its outer shell.

But my favourite was the young fisherman who drove away his soul by pursuing a forbidden love – the little Mermaid, who took him to live with her under the sea. He sent his soul away without a heart, so that it grew cruel, and in the end betrayed him. And how simple, how absurdly simple, when wealth and power had failed, was the temptation with which the soul enticed the young man away from his love – a girl who danced with naked feet, with feet "like little white pigeons".

... He remembered that the little Mermaid had no feet and could not dance. And a great desire came over him ...

But he went back to his love in the end, and they died together, and beautiful white flowers grew from their grave. What were you thinking of, Oscar, when you wrote that story? Was it not the love of men in conflict with the love of women? It is strange, is it not, what prophetic images the imagination can throw up …

You also inscribed for me a copy of *Lord Arthur Savile's Crime* – "Constance from Oscar, July '91" – I still have that. I loved that story also, in a morbid sort of way. I was quite surprised, on looking through it recently, to find that I marked some passages – among others, this: *Most men and women are forced to perform parts for which they have no qualifications.*

Strange, isn't it? I must have been searching your writing for clues, or perhaps I should say reassurances, that you knew what I knew – that we were in the middle of a charade, a game of "let's pretend". *Pretend that you see no change in me, and I will pretend that nothing has changed.* That was the long and the short of it, more or less.

10th of March 1898
Nervi

Oscar, you have no right to ask Carlos Blacker to "intercede" with me for more money. How you abuse the kindness of a good friend! Saying that your only fault was that you loved too much, and that any love is better than hate! So you are taking refuge under the guise of "one that loved not wisely, but too well", are you? Well, I am certainly no Desdemona, and I hardly think *he* is either! But it is typical of you.

And in any case, I do not agree; I do not agree that any love is better than hate. There is a kind of love that is more destructive, more poisonous, more degrading than honest cold hatred, and that is the love that makes a Moloch of the beloved and sacrifices everything to him: wife, children, career, self-respect. A Moloch is what *he* is in my eyes. No words can describe the loathing I have for him.

Hatred, Oscar, what do you know of it? You have not an ounce of viciousness in you. You may have lacerated with your tongue but you have never nurtured malice in your heart, as I have. How would you know to compare love with hate? To have hated just one person has been enough for me, and it is unfortunate, is it not, that it had to be the one you loved. It was after that summer in Worthing that I learned all about hatred. I wished him in Hell then, and I still think him a likely candidate for eternal damnation, if there is such a thing. I mean I wished it seriously, Oscar; have you ever seriously wished Hell upon a fellow man? I doubt it. I would have laid down my life, I swear it, if I thought it would make him suffer. My one wish was to expose him in the eyes of the world, to see him universally despised, cast out, laid low in the gutter where he belongs. Instead of which ... and now I hear that he is received and entertained in the best society, both in Rome and Nice, while you ...

I will confess something to you, Oscar. Last September, when I finally realised that you had joined him in Naples instead of coming here to me, I solemnly prepared to curse him. I trust this doesn't surprise you, from one who was once an initiate of the Hermetic Order of the Golden Dawn?

Qui Patitur Vincit – "He Who Endures, Conquers" is the usual translation, but I have long had my own: "She Who Suffers, Wins." Well, I was suffering then, and suddenly it all came back to me - my knowledge of the power generated by a focused, unmitigated, energised ill-wish. I was well aware of the risks, of course, but I thought that there was nothing I would not sacrifice to achieve my revenge on that boy – until I remembered the children.

Whatever you send, returns three times - that was something the Order continually impressed upon us, and the thought that any evil I might send could rebound upon our children was the only thing that stopped me. I did not care for myself. And I did not care for you, Oscar, even though I knew that you'd already suffered above and beyond what any civilised person could call just. That is the trouble with hate – it eclipses almost everything. Rather like love.

2nd of February 1892

Have been feeling very low all day, as I have been ever since we heard about Margaret. I just cannot believe that she is gone, and so suddenly - none of us even knew she was ill! - it has been nearly a month now, and I still cannot take it in. I suppose it is a blessing to go quickly, without protracted suffering or pain – but I hope, when my time comes, that I will at least have time to say goodbye to those I love. I cannot believe I will never see her again – a lioness amongst women, and a dear, dear friend.

It has been raining constantly, which has not helped. The children have been noisy, the house looks shabby and untidy. What an awful time of year this is, with no signs of Spring yet to give one hope, no glimmers of resurrection.

Oh, I know what I should do – I should dedicate myself to carrying on Margaret's work, in tribute to her dear, brave spirit. But I have not even been able to bring myself to visit Marylebone Road, knowing that she is not there. I think I feel guilty for having allowed Georgina to eclipse her so swiftly in my affections – not that she ever showed the least resentment, bless her. But what else could I do? I had to follow my heart, which is not stout enough to be always at the forefront of battle, and longs for rest and spiritual nourishment.

Georgina is my sole comfort now. She is my true Mother, everything my own mother should have been and wasn't, wise, kind and loving, like dear Mama Mary. And she is never surprised or scandalised by anything I tell her. She knows me so well, and Oscar too – she describes him as "a special blend of Irish innocence and English arrogance", which I think is true. She greatly admires him, but she worries – mainly on my account, which is sweet of her – about his indulgence of his young men. She has, of course, read both "Dorian" and "The Portrait of Mr W.H." and she worries – unnecessarily, I'm sure – about his reputation. She tells me to keep him close, but that is hardly ever possible nowadays! And I know Oscar - he is much too reliant upon society's admiration to risk anything that would make him fall foul of it in a serious way, and so naturally fastidious that I'm sure he would never indulge in anything sordid.

At the moment he is greatly involved in the rehearsals for "Lady Windermere", for he has pinned his hopes upon it, and says that this at last will make us a lot of money - I will believe that when I see it! - but I am hoping to persuade him to take a holiday this summer, I mean a proper family holiday with me and the boys, somewhere rural and peaceful and far from the madding crowd that he so loves...

23rd of April 1892

Is it not strange how good fortune, like bad, never comes singly, but seems to attract more to itself?   I know it sounds terrible to refer to poor Aunt Emily's death as "good fortune", but really one cannot deny that it was a merciful release for her, and since it leaves me the richer by £3,000 I cannot pretend to be desolate!   But in any case, the main good fortune has come from O.'s success with "Lady W." - the play is going from strength to strength! I knew from the first night that it would be so, for I felt the air all a-tingle with success, and I know that O. and his friends felt it too – how right we were to take no notice of the critics!   This has been the breakthrough we have been waiting for; and it was wonderful to see O. on top form, and riding so high. Now we have been able to pay off our debts, and it looks as though our penny-pinching days are finally over.   I feel rather ashamed to think that sordid financial gain should effect such a change in my spirits, but I do feel so much better – I have finally managed to clamber out of my Slough of Despond. I suppose it proves once and for all that I am not of the same mettle as Margaret; not destined for the same sort of life.

 O. has been so good to me recently – success makes him generous.   We have been making all sorts of plans, starting with a holiday abroad this summer, and continuing perhaps with a move to a larger house – oh, it would be wonderful to make a new start, in new surroundings! It has seemed so cramped here recently now that the boys are older. If "Salome" proves as great a success as "Lady W.", we will certainly be able to afford a larger establishment.

 O. is away at the moment, visiting Lord Alfred at Oxford. He had to leave at short notice, following an urgent telegram – all very mysterious, but I have made him promise to bring Lord A. back with him for a visit, as he is always such charming company…

29th of June 1892

O. has still not returned home after being out all night. Nothing unusual in that, of course, but I do hope he has not been doing anything foolish – he has worked himself up into such a state about "Salome". Last night he would speak of nothing but leaving the country, and renouncing England completely. He is totally disillusioned with the artistic climate here, and I must say I am tempted to agree, for it really is too ridiculous that the Lord Chamberlain should place a ban on something of the calibre of "Salome" just because it deals with Biblical characters. If O. were a painter or a sculptor, he would of course be free to choose whatever subject material he liked. It really is too stupid and narrow-minded for words.

 Miss Bernhardt is very angry, as well she might be,

having put in so much time, and some of her own money too, for the production. I have not seen her since the news broke, but O. has; I expect she will not stay long in England now. I shall miss her occasional visits here – at first I thought she had no time for me, but of late I have come to like her better.

At any rate, the censor cannot prevent publication in book form, and I am hoping that O. will apply his energies to that rather than planning to emigrate to France!

4th of July 1892

Received today a letter from Georgina, all kindness and solicitude, saying that of course the boys and I will be welcome at Babbacombe Cliff for the summer, and also to stay on when she goes abroad in September if we have no success in booking a family holiday. But I am determined to get O. to spend some time with us next month, when he returns from Bad Homburg rested and refreshed. He has been working so hard, and the furore over "Salome" has agitated him so ... He left yesterday, with Lord Alfred – so he is not alone, and I have made Bosie promise to look after him, and to ensure that he really does rest. They will both join us, hopefully, at whichever rural retreat I can book at short notice, and that is something to look forward to, especially for the boys. They already adore Bosie, Cyril particularly; and he always has time and patience for them, unusual in so young a man. He and O. make up the most fantastical games for them, always full of dragons, unicorns, hidden treasure and what not – I have sometimes laughed myself silly just watching them, as though they were all four little boys together.

He said to me only two days ago – Lord A., that is - when we were alone in the drawing room, "I don't know who to envy most, Constance, you or Oscar – or maybe it is the boys I envy – you are so charming "en famille", really, I wish I were one of you."

I told him, of course, that he must consider himself always as "one of us", since he was always welcome, and that I would be happy to look on him as part of the family. He seemed so pleased, and took my hand in both of his – he seemed about to say something more, when Oscar returned – I wonder what he would have said? That is the first time, by the way, that he has called me "Constance".

Oh, there is plenty more of this sort of thing, all in much the same vein. It is "Lord Alfred" this, and "Bosie" that ... anyone would think it was I who was becoming infatuated, and looking back I can see that in a way, I was. While I dithered, and waited for you to return from Bad Homburg, I seem to have amused myself mainly by indulging in fantasies of expanding our family to include him in some way. Just how I imagined this to be possible, or how I thought it would work, I mercifully cannot now remember. I had known him for just a year, and seen him only occasionally, almost always in your company. I knew just four things about him: that he was beautiful, aristocratic, an artist (or so he claimed), and that he adored you. I had little idea as yet how far you returned this adoration – that was to become clear over the next few months. But because he was charming, because he was new, I did all that I could to make him like me. I told him amusing anecdotes about you, I encouraged and applauded his opinions on art and the theatre, I expressed sympathy for his mother (to whom I was still hoping to be introduced) over his father's ill-treatment of her, and I let him know whenever I could that I understood and approved of his feelings for you. I hoped, I suppose, that he would think me exceptional, a woman of liberality, wit and perception; looking back, I can see that he must have thought me a great fool. And a fool is what I was. I told him that I liked him better than any of your other friends, and that I thought him a good influence upon you!

It has occurred to me since, that I was not so much trying to win his approval as to gain yours through my courting of it. Unconsciously I must already have been aware of how vital he was likely to become to you, and of how utterly I was in danger of losing you.

You returned home in August, oppressed by good health and determined to compensate for the frugality which the good doctors had forced upon you. Nevertheless, I was determined that we should have our family holiday, and accordingly we left for Cromer on the 20th of August to spend three weeks at Grove Farm – an idyllic country retreat, which at first seemed to promise everything I'd hoped for.

"The only thing I fear," I wrote to Georgina, "is that Oscar will get bored to death, but we have heaps of room and can ask people down to cheer him up..." For "people", of course, read Bosie.

He arrived at the beginning of September, hastily ousting poor Arthur Clifton and his new wife, and you and he played golf together, and entertained the boys, and we all had our photos taken, and everything seemed perfectly fine. When, at the end of the week, I left with the children to visit Georgina at Babbacombe, you asked to stay on for a few days, to have solitude to work on your new play. I left in the morning, and he was to take the London train in the afternoon – at least, that is what you both told me. But he didn't leave, did he Oscar? That very afternoon, he was "suddenly taken ill" and was obliged to stay on at Cromer. When you wrote and told me of this, I naively offered to return myself, in order to take care of him while you concentrated upon your work. But my telegrams went unanswered, and of course nothing could have been further from your desires than that I should intrude upon your time alone together. As I suffered the humiliation of waiting for a telegram that never came, it finally dawned upon me that I was not wanted – and with that came the realisation that all Bosie's fawning flattery, his compliments towards me, his assiduous courting of my approval, were nothing but gilt and air, designed to "keep me sweet" whilst he pursued the real object of his desire. And then slowly, slowly, as Georgina left for the Continent and that interminable, lonely autumn wore on, my feelings towards him, and my opinion of your friendship, changed utterly.

15th of March 1898
Nervi

I have just been reading Arthur Symons' review of your Ballad in the *Saturday Review*. The Ranee brought it to me – she has a copy sent regularly. It is a handsome compliment to your work, is it not? I hope you have read it. He says that you touch upon "the obscure deaths of the heart" - a beautiful description. *Yet each man kills the thing he loves* - I think he understands the poem, Oscar, as I do. I have been reading it again … one can have so many "deaths of the heart" in a lifetime, and in the end the death of the body seems but a small thing - do you feel this? Do you also feel, Oscar, that your life is really over, that you are just marking time, waiting for a death that has been delayed, as though a train you were expecting has been cancelled and you are left kicking your heels at the station, waiting for the next one? That is how I feel at the moment. I know it sounds morbid. It is partly because I feel so ill ...

Oh, if only I could find peace of mind! The weather is beautiful here. Each day is exquisite. There is a white lilac tree in the garden – it will blossom any day now. The white flowers that I used so to love oppress me now. I cannot get away from them. Sometimes I feel as though I am *made* of white flowers, so fragile on the surface, while underneath there are thorns, and hooks, and talons. That is what my skeleton will be, Oscar, hooks and talons. That is how I will be remembered – insipid on the surface, vindictive beneath. That is the sum total of my obituary.

20th[th] of March 1898
Nervi

I am feeling better now. Since I last sat at this
typewriter, I've had three days of bed rest. The
Ranee and Maria have been my only companions,
and poor Margaret is at a loss to understand what it
is that has been exhausting me so. I have been
forbidden to do any more photography! They do
not know about this epistle, but Maria hears me at
the typewriter and thinks I am writing a novel. She
tells me there will be plenty of time to write when I
am better. She sets great store by this operation,
which I am due to have next month. I must say I
am not looking forward to it, but really there seems
to be no alternative, as I am getting worse and
worse. I will not go into the nature of the operation
– you won't want to know, Oscar - but Dr Bossi is
convinced that the problem is cause by fibroids in
the womb compressing the nerves of the thigh.
Quite why this should also be affecting my arms
and face I cannot work out, but since the previous
operation I underwent at Dr Bossi's hands did result
in a welcome, though temporary, release from my
pain I am going to put myself once more in his care.
The Blackers are encouraging me to undergo the

procedure, and Carrie says she will come to Genoa to be with me during my convalescence, which is something to look forward to.

What do you look forward to, Oscar? If only you would take up your pen again, I really think you could retrieve all … or do you only look back, like me? That is perhaps a cruel question. Carlos writes discreetly of your lifestyle in Paris - I hear that you are frequently humiliated by old friends refusing to recognise you on the streets, in cafes. It makes me livid to hear that *he* is still received in the best society while you are thus outcast - in heaven's name, Oscar, doesn't it make *you* livid?

My reminiscences have reached that winter in Babbacombe when you finally joined us – not, as you'd promised, in the November for Vyvyan's birthday, but in the December, by which time I was thoroughly depressed.

22nd of September 1892
Babbacombe Cliff

The morning post has arrived, and still no word from O. - only a rather tedious letter from Aunt Mary Napier telling me in detail all about her plans for a European tour early next Spring. Poor thing, I think she is a little nervous of travelling alone, and has no-one to talk it over with. I shall write an encouraging reply.

There is definitely a chill of Autumn in the air today – the locals say the Autumn Tides are due, whatever they are – the leaves are turning, and it is very beautiful here, though there is a whiff of sadness about the place because of course Georgina has gone away. It was very kind of her to lease her home to us while she winters abroad, but it is not the same without her, and O. says now that he will not be able to join us until November. And I have no idea where he is, or with whom, though he mentions in his last letter that he has been invited to stay with Lady Queensberry in Bracknell next month – an invitation that surely should have included me!

The boys ask every day when their Papa is coming. I tell them to be good children and mind "Mademoiselle",who is finding them quite a handful I know - poor Miss Squine! I tell them that they will never be as clever and famous as their Papa if they do not mind their governess and work hard at their lessons; but why should they wish to emulate a father whom they hardly ever see? Cyril, who is such a sensitive little soul, asked me yesterday whether I was getting lonely.

"Well, everyone feels lonely from time to time, darling," I replied. "But you know, I have plenty of friends to cheer me up. Of course, I miss Aunty Georgina -"

"I meant Papa! Don't you feel lonely without Papa? Wouldn't you rather have <u>him</u> here, with <u>his</u> friends?"

Poor little fellow. He does miss O. so, and what is more he knows that I am unhappy. I thought that it did not show, but obviously it is apparent to Cyril, if not to Vyvyan who seems to accept the situation with his usual lack of curiosity.

25th of November 1892
Babbacombe

Received another letter from Aunt Mary today, asking me outright whether I would like to join her on her European holiday, and offering to pay my expenses! She says she is sure it would do me good, though who can have told her that I need good done to me I do not know. At any rate, it is most generous of her, and I shall consider it.

O. has still not arrived. I have been passing the time in reading Dante's "Inferno", and as I wrote to Georgina the other day, I feel myself lost in that "dark and bitter forest". Oh, I wish she were here, to comfort and uplift me with her wise, kind words and spiritual advice!

5th of December 1892
Babbacombe

Well, Oscar is finally here. He is down on the beach with the boys, making sandcastles. Sandcastles, in December! He has brought some tin soldiers as a belated birthday present for Vyvyan, which has naturally delighted both the boys. He has been in Paris, apparently – I didn't ask with whom. I think he has quarrelled with Bosie, because of the way he reacted when I asked after him, and when I tried to press him further, he became touchy and suspicious.

"What?" he responded irritably, "Why do you want to know? Who has been speaking to you about him behind my back?"

"No-one," I replied, much astonished.

"You have been writing to Lady Queensberry, haven't you?"

"Certainly not. Why should I write to Lord Alfred's mother about her son? I have never even met her!" (I am still smarting to think that I was not included in the invitation to Bracknell).

"Then why should you make such an accusation?"

"I have not made any accusation!" I protested, feeling certain that something very serious must have occurred. How I hate being in the dark like this! But there is no reasoning with O. about anything at the moment. If he and Bosie have quarrelled, perhaps that is a good thing, as he will finally be able to concentrate upon his writing. I must try and put Bosie out of my mind.

On the subject of O.'s writing, I had a charming letter from Robbie Ross the other day, enquiring after the progress of "Mrs Arbuthnot", as he calls the new play – O. says he is going to change the title to "A Woman Of No Importance" without letting anyone know until the first night, such nonsense. The letter was addressed exclusively to me, and in the most friendly terms, asking after my health and that of the boys. I am thinking of inviting him to join us here for a while - I believe he is a much better friend to O. than Bosie, after all.

14th of January 1893
Babbacombe

O. left for Paris today, and I'm afraid we did not part on very friendly terms. I am feeling wretched. This Torquay holiday has not been a success for either of us. When I think of all the dreams and plans I had last Spring – a family holiday, a new house, and all that foolish indulgence of A.D. - well, I am ashamed of my own naivety.

The only enjoyable days I have spent over the winter season were those when Robbie was here, and even then I was not sorry that his visit was brief, for it was embarrassing for him to see how badly O. and I get along at the moment. He is a sensitive soul, and is torn between his longstanding friendship with O. and disapproval of the way he treats me. At least he does not automatically side with him. The constant interchange of letters and telegrams with A.D. was very obvious, and spoke for itself. I am glad, by the way, that I did not ask Robbie what he thinks of him, as I'd intended to do – it would have offended his natural delicacy. Dear Robbie, he is so warm-hearted and well-meaning – he is certainly the far better friend.

At least the boys did not see us quarrel. They have so much enjoyed having their Papa here, and are heartbroken to see him go. Of course it is easier to convince a child that Paris is the only place where one can edit the French version of "Salome" than it is to convince a wife ... and he will have to keep his promise to be back here by the middle of February, for he knows that I leave at the end of the month and he quite agrees that we cannot leave the boys with poor Miss Squine for too long.

I have written this morning to Aunt Mary to confirm the arrangements. I am determined to have a proper holiday at last, even if it has to be as companion to Aunt M! The boys are quite happy to stay here, I think; they have become very attached to Babb, and do not seem to miss London at all, or ask when we will be returning to Tite Street. I will have to think seriously about their schooling this year. Very soon they'll both be old enough to be sent away ...

Yes, that was a low point in our marriage - not the first low point, of course, but it marked a change in my attitude to our unspoken agreement. For one thing, I was no longer prepared to turn a blind eye to your extravagance, your self-indulgence and your neglect; for another, I was no longer silent in the face of your excuses.

We'd made a whirlwind visit to London, you'll remember, right at the beginning of the year. The lease on Tite Street was due to expire in June, and I was anxious to initiate the search for a new house – but you would have none of it, insisting that we had plenty of time, that it could all be sorted out when I returned from Italy. So instead we filled the days with visits to long-neglected friends and relatives – chief amongst them, of course, your mother.

It was at Oakley Street that we dined with the Leversons – do you remember? I had met them both before of course, but always in mixed company, at the theatre or at literary soirées. This was a more intimate occasion. At the end of the meal we ladies retired, leaving you, your brother and Ernest Leverson to your cigars, port and unsavoury anecdotes. A dreary affair you must have found it, I imagine, with none of your set to entertain you, or be entertained – I'll wager you can't remember what the three of you talked about when we left the table. I, on the other hand, can remember *our* conversation almost verbatim.

What an interesting triad we were – three literary women of the modern era (I did still think of myself then as a "literary woman"), with you in common. If I once compared you to the moon, Oscar, then surely we were the Triad of the Moon: Speranza, of course, the Mother, the matriarch *par excellence*; I the Maiden, because in spite of my wifely and motherly experience I still did not know who I was, or what I was supposed to be doing with my life; and Mrs Ada Leverson, with her long face, hooded eyes, and dry, cynical humour, seemed to have bypassed both phases, and been born a Crone. I found her inscrutability disconcerting. You must have experienced something of the same reaction, for you always called her "The Sphinx".

"How interesting," she began, "to see Oscar amongst his family. He is so very different from when I see him amongst his friends. Here, he is quite restrained and responsible, the dutiful husband, son and father!"

She waited, with head inclined and a sly smile on her lips, to see how I would take this remark. Was it a compliment on my wifely influence, or an implication that she knew more about my husband that I did? I managed a brittle laugh.

"You would not think him restrained if you could see him at home, Mrs Leverson, playing with the boys! He is not so much the dutiful father as the boisterous playmate, and quite an irresponsible one at that!"

"Oh! When playing with boys, I'm sure he is in his element."

There was my answer, and I bridled at the sheer arrogance of her attempt to make witticisms at my expense in the presence of my mother-in-law. Speranza, however, seemed oblivious.

"Restrained ..." she mused. "Restriction of any kind has always been anathema to Oscar. Ever since he was a little boy, he was always so headstrong; the slightest setback would bring on a flood of tears. Of course, it shows the sensitive and artistic nature," she continued, filling sherry glasses from the decanter upon the sideboard and arranging them on a tray; "Willie was much more pliant. I used to think his willingness to please the sign of a thoughtful nature, but now I see it as a defect; he is too easily led. Oscar was always full of noise and protest, the sign of a restless, creative spirit. Like my own."

I accepted my glass with a smile; Leverson raised

an eyebrow, and a corner of her mouth.

"The spirit of our age is a restless one, I think, Lady Wilde. It is the last decade of the century. A *fin de siècle* is always a time of upheaval – socially, spiritually, individually. That is why we find ourselves picking fretfully at the seams of our restrictive society – half unconsciously, perhaps."

She may have a nice turn of phrase, I thought spitefully, but Speranza will be a match for her. Your mother however, sinking into her chair with a full glass and a sigh, was back in Ireland.

"Half unconsciously? No! There must be nothing half-hearted about the overturning of oppression, Mrs Leverson! Nations and individuals alike – and a nation is made up of individuals, and yet is itself like one individual with its own particular character, its habits, its peculiar virtues and vices – no nation and no individual should be forced to suffer the imposition of an alien character, the suppression of its very soul. I feel within myself, Mrs Leverson, the sufferings of my poor country – *Ireland*," she emphasised, should that lady be under any misapprehension.

Her guest nodded slowly, and Speranza launched into a brief history of her girlhood, and the discovery of her twin vocation as poetess and Hope of the Nation.

"I was a priestess at the altar of Freedom ..."

I had heard it all before, which is not to say that I was unsympathetic; I remembered that Mrs Leverson was Jewish, and wondered how this ode to national identity and popular martyrdom struck her.

"Then my wild soul entered the prison of woman's destiny..."

This was your mother's usual description of her marriage, and I mused once again that whereas I had married to spread my wings, she had found hers clipped by the experience. Who would she have been, I wondered, if she had never married – if there had been no Oscar, no Willie? For now she lived through her sons ... I could not imagine her a spinster, she was too opulent. That day she wore dark red velvet, and a headdress embroidered with little jet beads. Earlier, you had muttered to me that she had the look of a pair of curtains. She always brought out the Irish in you, Oscar, in both speech and humour.

I smiled again, and caught Mrs Leverson's eye upon me. I was afraid she would think me contemptuous of my mother-in-law – many did find her ridiculous, I knew, but how could I feel anything other than admiration for a woman who exuded such a strong and positive identity? She had never for one moment stood in her husband's shadow – she had created herself in her own image. Could I do that, I wondered, or have I left it too late? I too am Irish, on my mother's side ...

But we were not talking about Ireland any more; how long had my mind been wandering?

"To impose the strictures of society upon the individual – you regard this as an impertinence? Or did you mean, when you spoke of "imposing an alien character", the tyranny of one individual over another, in parallel to the tyranny of one nation over another?"

Mrs Leverson had actually managed to turn the conversation – no small feat, when your mother was rehearsing her autobiography.

"Oh! Most certainly I was referring to the strictures of society. But the artist will always soar above them. The artist has an obligation to search for his – or her – own destiny, outside of the petty mores of bourgeois convention."

"Oscar would agree with you there, I think."

"Of course he would. He is so like me, Mrs Leverson. He inherits my character. Willie is more like his father. Perhaps that is why I can live with Willie, whereas I could never tolerate life with Oscar. Constance, how ever do you manage it?"

Mrs Leverson turned towards me indulgently, and I realised that I had made only one comment so far, and that relating to the nursery.

"Why, as to that," I said, summoning my wits and determining not to let that woman underestimate me, "we have little opportunity to become intolerant with one another whilst each pursuing our own interests. We support one another, of course – I support Oscar's career in every way that I can – but I do think it important for a wife to have her own resources, her own interests and activities. Even if she is married to a genius."

Speranza nodded approvingly, and Mrs Leverson responded, somewhat offhandedly, "Oh yes - Oscar mentioned your association with Lady Mount-Temple, and you were also a disciple of the late Lady Sandhurst were you not? You are in favour of female suffrage, I assume?"

"Most certainly I am!"

"And Oscar? What is his opinion on the issue?"

How determined she was to turn the conversation back to you! I favoured her with a small, tight smile. "You must ask him that yourself, Mrs Leverson. He will no doubt give you a witty reply, to hide the fact that he views the prospect with real apprehension."

"Oh, Constance, of course he does not! He is a great supporter of female emancipation; if he were not, he would be neither my son nor your husband!"

"He pays lip service to the idea, Mama, certainly; but I think he regards the prospect of any real social upheaval as rather vulgar." I laughed, to show that I meant to be witty rather than critical. Mrs Leverson now became quite animated.

"Do you? Do you really? Do you know, I am tempted to agree. And for himself, he likes to live dangerously, does he not?"

"If society were suddenly to become unconventional, *en masse*, he would be constrained to adopt the strictest conservatism simply in order to be different."

Ah, now she regarded me with a new respect! But she was still not quite sure how much I knew.

"You seem to have a good understanding of your husband, Mrs Wilde," she ventured; I gave an amused shrug.

"Well, I should hope I do, Mrs Leverson, as you no doubt have a good understanding of yours!"

Here Speranza interjected: "Oscar is very fortunate in Constance, Mrs Leverson, and what's more he knows it. To know all is to forgive all, as I have often said regarding Sir William, God rest his soul. Though of course his behaviour was quite different from Oscar's."

This caused Mrs Leverson to regard her also with a new respect, though she had only meant to imply that unlike your father, you did not harbour a mistress.

"Well! It must be quite enlivening to have an unconventional husband. Ernest, I'm afraid, is thoroughly respectable. I am obliged to invent vices for him just to amuse myself, as he seems to have none of his own. I rather envy you, Mrs Wilde. I can just envisage myself as the wife of an artist."

"Say rather, an artist in your own right, Mrs Leverson!" admonished Speranza; and she concurred, "Yes, that too"; but her eye was upon me. I remembered that she wrote for *Punch*, and was casting around for a suitable reference to my own modest literary output when she suddenly asked, "Did you know Oscar well, Mrs Wilde, before you married him?"

This, I felt, was downright impertinence, and the use of your Christian name in contrast with her formal address to myself was beginning to grate considerably.

"Please," I said through gritted teeth, "do call me Constance. Yes, I think I knew him pretty well, but obviously over the course of a marriage one discovers more about one's spouse as the years go by, and the layers peel back. Do you not find the same with Mr Leverson?"

"Oh, Ernest is so boring. He seems to have no layers at all. I was only nineteen when I married him; and do you know, after nearly twelve years of matrimony I still find myself confused as to its true nature and purpose!"

"Oh!" cried Speranza, galvanised, "It took me the whole of my marriage to discover that Woman's true destiny can be achieved neither within matrimony, nor apart from it!"

This was an enigmatic and potentially shocking line of speculation, but since I already knew that your mother regarded Woman's true destiny as one of heroic suffering in one form or another, I was determined to bypass it. I rose, and offered to pour some more sherry; both ladies held out their glasses with alacrity. As I approached Mrs Leverson she asked casually, "What do you think of Lord Alfred Douglas, Constance?"

I kept a firm grip upon the decanter, and managed to refresh her glass without spilling a drop before replying steadily, "He is a charming young man, but a little too inclined to waste both Oscar's time and his own. Oscar never gets any work done when Lord Alfred is around."

"I have not met him," commented Speranza, "but I hear tales of his extravagance. I hope it will not rub off upon Oscar, as I already have enough trouble with Willie in that respect. I know his mother slightly – poor Lady Queensberry, she is a charming woman, but she does tend to *languish* so. I know she has had a difficult time with the divorce and all that it entails, but a woman of spirit should rise above such things. One would have thought that to be rid of such a brutish husband as hers would give her a new lease of life!"

"Yes, he *is* extravagant, and not only with money," said Mrs Leverson, completely ignoring the latter part of your mother's speech. "He has got himself into several scrapes, I hear, from which friends have been obliged to extricate him. He has no sense of discretion. You are right to be distrustful, Constance."

Anxiety began to stir within me. "What sort of scrapes?"

Mrs Leverson gave me what I believe is called a "speaking look" from beneath carefully raised eyebrows. "Oh, indiscretions, mainly. He got into trouble a few months ago, over some letters written while he was at Oxford. It was Oscar's generosity that saved him on that occasion, as perhaps you know."

"No," I said steadily, "I did not know. But then Oscar is always generous towards his friends."

"Oh, that is like him!" agreed Speranza. "There was a lady in the case?" (In her day, the term "indiscretion" could mean nothing else.)

"No, no lady in *this* case," said Mrs Leverson, looking at me very directly; and I remembered how suddenly you had left for Oxford back in May, and felt the anger and resentment I had been controlling all evening surge up within me – how was it possible that this woman knew more about you and Bosie than I did?

At that point we heard masculine laughter ascending the stairs, and I was relieved – suddenly I longed for your presence, and for some reassurance.

"Ladies! Are you feeling neglected? We have been wandering amongst thorns whilst you, I hope, have been dallying in rose gardens. We have been criticising the critics. What have you been discussing? Come, do admit it, you have been talking about us behind our backs, have you not?"

"No dear," said Speranza complacently, determined not to admit anything of the sort, "we have been talking about ourselves. Why must men always assume that women have no better topic of conversation than their husbands?" Ada Leverson said nothing, but greeted you with a slow, Sphinx-like smile.

"Goodnight, Constance," she said when we parted. "It has been such a pleasure. I do hope we will meet again soon, for I feel we have so much in common."

I murmured something polite. I was glad that I would soon be out of London, indeed out of the country. This woman, who seemed to have an entrée to your private world, had unsettled me more thoroughly than any of your male friends.

It was only much later, as I was falling asleep, that I remembered that she had never reciprocated my courtesy and invited me to call her "Ada".

23rd of March 1898
Nervi

All this talk of the Leversons has unsettled me yet again. I remember that brief visit I paid you, Oscar, when you were staying with them during the trial because no hotel would accommodate you. It should have been I who sheltered you, should it not, in your hour of need? But my family had already intervened … and I had the boys to think of … and even Robbie had advised against it. I pleaded and pleaded with you to flee the country, but you would have none of it. Whether through arrogance or through misguided optimism, you were determined to face your fate – and I, who had already deserted you when you most needed my support, had no power to persuade you.

It is not pleasant to think that Ada Leverson was your confidante and comfort at that time instead of me. She was the Sphinx who knew all your secrets, whereas I – well, what did I know, exactly? That is a question I keep returning to.

I enjoyed my Continental holiday much more than I had anticipated – for one thing, in the event it was not just myself and Aunt Mary Napier; we were joined by her daughter Lizzie, and my other cousin Lilias, both welcome company on our forays around

Florence and Rome. And I had my new Kodak with me, so was able to take pictures, as well as study Rennaissance Art and attend Mass whenever I liked, in beautiful Churches (and finally in St Peter's itself!) How I longed to become a Catholic then - I loved the ritual, the sacrifice, the continual offer of forgiveness – I was not even sure what I needed forgiveness for, but I longed to enter the darkness of the confessional and emerge cleansed, renewed, absolved. I reflected upon the aesthetic excesses of our early married life, our flaunting of our home as the House Beautiful and of ourselves as children of the *fin de siècle*, and wondered why I had allowed you to make me play this part, for which I had no qualifications. I wished that I could step out of my past and discard it like a stained and tattered garment, and for a brief time it really did seem possible that I could move from the limbo of the voyager into any life I chose – a quiet life where there were no hidden rocks, no sickening thud and tear as the soft underbelly of my pretensions was struck aground. I told myself that I might never go home; that I could change my name, perhaps even change my nationality, send for the children – but there I always stopped. There was so much of you in our sons – how could I take them from you?

Yes, you may well be surprised to read this, Oscar, for since then I *have* changed our children's name, and kept them from you, and given them Adrian Hope as a guardian. It is ironic, is it not, that I once contemplated as a free choice the course of action that would later be forced upon me by disgrace and despair?

And then when I returned to London, you were not at the station to meet me, even though I had telegraphed in advance; you were not at Tite Street, which I found cold and desolate, with a mountain of unopened post upon the hallstand. You were at the Savoy with Bosie, and you had no intention of coming home.

21st of April 1893

Well, it looks as though "A Woman Of No Importance" is going to do every bit as well as "Lady Windermere". Although O. had to face a few catcalls on the first night (the public have never forgiven him for coming onstage with that cigarette after "Lady W."), last night put the seal of success upon it, I think, with the Prince of Wales in the Royal Box. The P.o.W. was delighted with the play, apparently – as well he might be, since he is known to take a personal interest in sins of the flesh. He spoke privately with O. afterwards, and apparently told him not to alter a single line. O. is of course on top form, and delighted with himself. He has now moved from the Savoy to the Albemarle, and I have not yet seen him in private.

He seems to think I should be particularly pleased with the play since it is written, he says, "from the woman's point of view". Well, it may be his idea of the woman's point of view, but from my point of view it has a remarkably similar array of characters to "Lady W." - the wicked aristocrat (always Lord

Henry Wootton by another name); the witty woman; the wronged woman; the good woman; and of course, the beautiful young man. We women, apparently, are supposed to have a much better time than men because "there are far more things forbidden to us than are forbidden to them". Oh, very Ada Leverson, if indeed it refers to women at all. One needs the luxury of choice, so seldom available to our sex, before one can enjoy the taste of forbidden fruit.

I don't know why I am so cynical about the play, since I am likely to reap some benefits of its undoubted success; but I have become very jaded since returning to London. And I really do not know what is to become of O. and me. I have hardly seen him since my return. I do not know what to do with his letters; I suppose I shall have to take them to him personally at the Albemarle, since I could not very well give them to him at the theatre!

It is lovely to have the children back. By all accounts they enjoyed themselves greatly at Babbacome, when Bosie joined them after I left. And Babb is _my_ place, mine and Georgina's ... I tried to seem pleased for them, but fear that I failed miserably.

25th of April 1893

I have just returned from delivering O.'s letters — quite a few of them by now. I went to the

Albemarle, only to be told that he "and Lord Alfred Douglas" had left yesterday, apparently after some disagreement with the hotel manager. I imagine that the disagreement was of a financial nature, for when the said gentleman eventually deigned to come and speak to me, he could hardly bring himself to tell me where they had gone. At last he said, "They <u>mentioned</u> that they were going back to the Savoy, Madam," oozing disapproval from every syllable, though whether of them or of the Savoy I am not certain. By the time I arrived there, I was close to tears and the whole thing went very badly.

They were staying in one of the best suites of course, and I was shown into the sitting room; but they were still in the bedroom, and the door was open. There was another gentleman present, and they were arguing, in French, about something to do with "Salome". When the boy announced me they all turned towards the door, very embarrassed, and O. apologised to the others in a low voice and came out to me in his dressing-gown. He was very abrupt with me at first, but seeing that I was upset, and no doubt wishing to avoid a scene, he became kinder.

"My letters! But how delightful to receive so many, and by special delivery! Tite Street? Is that really my address? Do you know, it is so long since I have been to Tite Street that I'd quite forgotten I have a house there! Thank you, my dear," (kissing me on the cheek) "for reminding me that I have an address, even as lesser mortals. Remember, O

Poet, thou too art human!"

The others emerged somewhat shamefacedly from the bedroom, and Bosie greeted me in a quiet, sulky manner and then introduced me to the French gentleman, since O. was too absorbed in reading his correspondence to do so. Monsieur Pierre Louys - I had never heard of him before. He seemed quite at a loss, which made me suspect that the ignorance was mutual. Bosie asked after the children, and I'm afraid I replied quite coldly, as I am now far from happy about his effect upon them. Evidently he was supposed to be studying during his stay at Babbacombe, and had even brought a tutor with him; but if Cyril is to be believed, he avoided his lessons at every opportunity, and encouraged my boys to do the same. Poor Miss Squine confirmed that she had a very difficult time with them while I was away. Of course, I have not been able to speak to O. about it.

After a while O. interrupted the conversation, waving an invitation card under Bosie's nose.

"Did you know about this, dear boy?"

Bosie took and read it, with some surprise. "Certainly not. I have not been invited myself! How very remiss of Mama. I shall telegraph her about it today, and ask what she means by it!"

"Probably she does not know where you are. There, Constance, it is not only I who deserve reproach; Lady Queensberry would no doubt sympathise with you. You have an errant husband, she an errant son."

"You're invited too, by the way, Constance," said Bosie carelessly, handing the card to me – and I intercepted a look of annoyance from O. as I took it. Sure enough, it was addressed to Mr and Mrs Oscar Wilde, and requested the pleasure of our company at Lady Queensberry's May Ball, to be held at Bracknell on the 19th. I am utterly convinced that O. would have gone without me, and never said a word about it.

"It is very kind of your mother, and I shall write and thank her," I said after an awkward silence. Bosie gave an enigmatic smile.

"But will you come, Constance?" His use of my Christian name, which I once thought so charming, was now beginning to grate on me.

I looked from him to my husband. O. looked uncomfortable and disapproving, Bosie sly and vicious. It dawned upon me that they had been having an argument, and that Bosie was endorsing his mother's invitation to me purely to cause chagrin. How dared either of them think to use me as a pawn in their sordid little game!

My first instinct was to refuse; but I have said that I will accept the invitation, and have undertaken to write to Lady Q. today on behalf of both O. and myself to that effect. Why, I wonder? I can hardly imagine that I will enjoy myself. Did I do it purely out of spite? Or am I just curious to meet Bosie's mother? I should like to meet her, if only to find out what she thinks of O. and of his friendship with her son. How much does she know, I wonder?

Yes, I admit it, I'm curious, and I am also spiteful. O. had no right to humiliate me this morning in front of his friends. I suppose he would say it was my fault, for turning up unannounced.

He bade me farewell in a very jovial manner.

"When are you coming home, Oscar?" I asked plainly.

"Home? Ah yes, to Tite Street! How I should love to visit Tite Street! They tell me I have a charming house there. Don't worry my dear, you shall certainly be seeing me at Tite Street sooner than you think. The rates these hotels charge are quite shocking, and perfectly respectable people are being forced to live at their own houses simply because they cannot afford to live anywhere else!"

I bade them all farewell, I hope reproachfully. M. Louys looked amazed, and quite upset. Yes, I think he was completely ignorant of my existence.

I could see the bedroom very clearly, by the way. There was but one bed. I can hardly believe that O. and Bosie have been sleeping quite openly <u>together in the same bed</u>. How could he do anything so blatant? Is he completely mad? Is he completely past caring what people will think of him? Is he past caring what people will think of <u>me</u>?

24th of March 1898
Nervi

So I *did* know, then. And yet I wrote earlier, and
believed it, that I had never imagined you and Bosie
in any sexual embrace before the events at
Worthing opened my eyes to the sordid mechanics
of the matter. What the eye doesn't see, the heart
doesn't grieve over – isn't that what they say? But I
remember now: I saw that bed, and all that it
implied, quite clearly. In a hotel! But fool that I
was, I seem not to have grasped the potential
consequences, worrying only "what people would
think." Some things have to be *brought home* to
one, do they not?

That was the last time that I asked you to come
home. After feeling so humiliated, I swore to
myself that I would never ask again; which was just
as well, for excepting those four brief months that
winter, the calm before the storm, you never really
did come home.

What is the use in going on with this? I will never
send it; you will never read it. I am in constant pain
now, and so tired. The keys of the typewriter feel
stiff and unwieldy.

Last night I had a terrible dream, the kind which
makes one afraid to go back to sleep: I dreamt that
I was turning into a doll. I could feel myself

stiffening all over, a creeping paralysis invading my limbs while at the same time I was outside of my body, watching the transformation.

My expression became fixed and glazed, my skin waxy and yellow, my movements jerky. I watched a tear slide slowly down my cheek. With the last movements of which I was capable, I tried to raise my hand to my mouth; and I watched in horror, knowing that I was going to pull out my tongue so that I should never be able to tell the story of what had happened to me, and how I used to be a real woman.

Even as I woke with my heart pounding, I realised that the dream did not make sense – for surely a doll would be tongueless in any case? But the memory of it has been with me all day. Is it a premonition of death? My death, and my silence? Rigor mortis, the work of the embalmer, all spring to mind. And is that how I am to be remembered, as a silent, lifeless doll?

Oh Oscar, I do not want to die without seeing you again. Will you not even write to me?

25th of March 1898
Nervi

I feel much better this morning, after a good (and dreamless) sleep. What do you think I have just received in the post? A letter from Robbie, very charming and friendly, giving me your Paris address (which I already had from Carlos Blacker, but he was not to know that); and with not a single request for money, which I greatly appreciate. I think, reading between the lines, that he is trying to encourage me to write to you – little knowing, of course, that I am spending my small store of energy doing just that!

He sent news of Aubrey Beardsley's death, "in case I had not heard" - and indeed, I had not. How awful! At the age of only twenty-six! That was my age when we married, when I thought that life was just beginning. I loved his pictures – I know that you liked to speak slightingly of his talent whenever you were at loggerheads, but I never faltered in my admiration. As for himself – well, I met him socially a few times, and he was *difficile*, as they say. He was often with his sister - she looked much but said little - I wonder what her story would be? No doubt she also has torn out her tongue.

Robbie ends his letter with "God bless you, Constance". He has been so good to us both, Oscar, I cannot believe that it was he who set your feet on the path to Hell. If you had contented yourself with

133

him, he would never have led you to the cliff's edge, and encouraged you to jump.

The other day I found the little pearl-coloured rosary that I had blessed by an old priest in Florence during my Italian holiday; it was stowed away in a corner of my last trunk, still in its kid purse. I slept with it under my pillow last night, and I'm sure it protected me. Robbie writes that you have been blessed by the Pope in Rome, and I remembered that I also, amongst the crowds that thronged St Peter's for the Jubilee Mass during that holiday, received that saintly old man's blessing. And yet you discouraged me from converting ... I wonder if you have since changed your mind ... though I suspect you are still too attached to your sins. Georgina used to say that the English would never return to the Catholic faith while it persisted in reminding them that God has a Mother... ah, but we are Irish, aren't we, Oscar?

I am rambling again, am I not? Do you see how this letter is degenerating? I sometimes fear that my physical weakness is softening my mind. I never leave the house now, Oscar. I rise early, but the exertion of rising leaves me so exhausted that after breakfast I must rest for an hour upon the chaise longue. I have it placed by the window, so that I can watch the world go by; not that there is much traffic passing from the town, but I watch the white lilac tree, and the rest of the garden. And then I seat myself at this typewriter. In the afternoon I may receive a visitor, usually the Ranee, who keeps me in touch with events in the outside world, and we take tea together. When I am alone again, I read my diaries. Now is not this the life of a widow? And who would have thought it? I, who was once Châtelaine of the House Beautiful!

Yesterday I read the following diary entry for 20th of May 1893:

Returned this morning from Bracknell. Lady Q.'s ball was very grand, and she herself an interesting character study — she cultivates an aura of childlike complaisance and wistfulness which fails to mask the fact that nearly everything she says and does is motivated by hatred of her former husband. While this is at least partly understandable, I do find it terrible that she encourages her children to feel the same. No wonder Bosie behaves in such an unbalanced way, if this is how he has been brought up! I think of my own little boys, how they adore O. and think him the best Papa in the world, and I have resolved once again to hide my grievance from them as best I can, and never to try to turn them against him. God forbid that I should ever take pride in saying "My sons hate their father!"

Well, I had not yet set eyes on Lord Queensberry then, of course. But through all that has happened, Oscar, I have kept that promise. I have never tried to turn the boys against you, even when friends and family encouraged me to. Oh Oscar, I never imagined that our sons would be anything other than proud to name you as their father!

I remember that ball so well. I can see myself now,

back in that high-ceilinged room with the dazzling chandeliers, the long French window, the genteel throng parading the floor; I am feeling absurdly nervous - is it really so long since I have been to a ball? I am clutching my fan in both hands, standing like a wallflower in the wings while you wander off to find Bosie. I am thinking "this is a part for which I have no qualifications..."

I feel a tap on my shoulder, and hear my mother's sharp admonition: *Constance! Don't do that!* But it is you.

"Don't do what, Oscar?" I say irritably, startled out of my nerves.

"Don't *stare*, my dear, at poor Arthur Humphreys. I agree that he is singularly unfortunate in his appearance, but what can one expect from the manager of Hatchards? And what on earth is he *doing* here? How very out of place he looks, rather like a dandelion amongst a spray of carnations – yet, a dandelion with a stoop. One puff of wind, and all his hair will fly off. He will be revealed as a puffball. Come, my dear, Bosie's mother is quite avid to meet you."

"I was not staring at anyone, Oscar!"

My vexation must show in my face, as I inadvertantly catch the eye of the tall, tow-headed gentleman who fits your uncharitable description. To my mortification, he blushes, and making a quick half-bow turns awkwardly away.

"Ah! Then it was he staring at you, which I like even less. Let us flee now, while he is looking the other way."

The crowd parts before us as we approach Bosie

and his mother. Lady Queensberry is tall and fair –
a gracious looking woman, who must once have
been beautiful, but who now looks just as your
mother described her – *languishing*. She droops on
her son's arm, a tight, sad smile on her lips. Her
eyes, though blue as forget-me-nots, are watery and
weak. Yes, she must certainly have suffered, I
think, but how she cultivates her aura of grief! She
is trying to look like a lost little girl. Her son must
owe much of his charm and mannerisms, as well as
his looks, to her.

"My dear Mrs Wilde, I am so delighted to meet
you at last! Ah, but you are every bit as beautiful as
they say, my dear, and what a charming dress!
Green does not suit every woman, does it? But it
suits you. Now, I am determined to have a few
minutes' talk with you, even at the risk of neglecting
my other guests. I have waited so long to meet you;
I am certainly not going to let you go with no more
than a "good evening". Boysie, you may go away
now. Come, my dear."

She takes me by both hands and leads me towards
the chairs. "Boysie" shrugs, and turns away; you
pat him on the arm in an avuncular manner, as if to
say *leave them to gossip – what harm can it do?*

It is difficult not to take an immediate dislike to a
woman who, having first complimented one on the
unfashionable colour of one's gown, then insists on
clasping both one's hands in an iron grip throughout
the conversation – however, I maintain my
composure, curious to know what she can have to
say to me. I imagine she wants to talk about her
son; but to my surprise, she launches upon a subject

which appears to have no relevance to me whatsoever – her former husband.

"I am so relieved, my dear," she begins, "that Boysie's father has not been causing any unpleasantness! I was so afraid that he might cause embarrassment to your husband. He behaves abominably, you know, to all his children's friends, and to mine. It is his mission to make life as unpleasant for all of us as possible."

I am quite taken aback by this outburst. "Why, Lady Queensberry," I falter, "as far as I know, Oscar has never met the Marquess. I am sure there would be no occasion for any unpleasantness."

"Oh, but there would be! He would make one! My dear, you can have no concept of that man's viciousness! Let me give you an example: our eldest son, Francis – that is, Viscount Drumlanrig – is, as you may know, private secretary to Lord Rosebery. Now, you would think that would make his father proud, would you not? But no! He has written the most fearful letters, full of dreadful accusations against poor Lord Rosebery – he has got it into his head that there is some ulterior motive for all his kindness, and encouragement of our son's career. Now, Queensberry may make as big a fool of himself as he likes, but I do not want another son's happiness to be jeopardized by his ridiculous behaviour. I would hate the same thing to happen regarding Boysie's friendship with your husband. Mr Wilde has been so good to him. I am in hopes that he will be a steadying influence, and encourage him to take an interest in his studies, or at least in something worthwhile. He has no direction in life, you see; he is inclined to be wilful, and somewhat hysterical. Well, I know myself what it is to have a nervous disposition, but I sometimes fear that Boysie may have inherited his father's temper. I pray not. Oh, it is terrible, *terrible* – you have no idea – you know he is planning to marry some poor, deluded little fool?"

"Lord Alfred?" I am astonished, and completely out of my depth.

"Lord Queensberry! He is engaged to a poor, innocent young woman who can have no conception of what his character really is, or she would never have consented to such a step. Oh, my heart bleeds for her! When I think of what she shall shortly have to endure at his hands!" (Here she actually releases one of mine, in order to place hers upon her bosom.)

Curious though I am, I am not bold enough to enquire into the nature of the second Lady Queensberry's forthcoming ordeal. Instead, I say, "Well, I do appreciate your concern for your sons, Lady Queensberry, but maybe their father will feel less inclined to interfere in their affairs when he has new domestic responsibilities to occupy him."

"Oh! Do not believe it for a second, Mrs Wilde! If once he takes it into his head to make trouble for your husband and Boysie, as he has done for poor Francis and Lord Rosebery, it will take more than a new wife to put him off the scent. Do you see?"

Suddenly, I am beginning to see. A tingle of apprehension touches my spine.

"Lady Queensberry," I say, "are you saying that your former husband has made *specific allegations* regarding Lord Drumlanrig and Lord Rosebery?"

"Oh ... no nothing specific, nothing specific. But it does not need to be, do you see? You do see, don't you?"

I find myself unable to reply. My lips are parted in horror, my expression frozen. I nod, dumbly. Lady Queensberry withdraws her other hand, and begins to glance around the room, and to nod and smile at various people.

"I am ignoring my other guests," she murmurs. "I am afraid, my dear, that out little *tête-à-tête* must come to an end. Think on what I have said. I shall introduce you to Lady Ashington, she will take care of you."

We rise, she with sad dignity, I in consternation. She pats my hand.

"It has been so lovely to meet you, my dear Mrs Wilde. I wish we'd had time to talk about your own little boys – Boysie tells me they are quite charming. And they are fortunate to have Mr Wilde for a father. My sons all hate their father, every one of them. That is what he has brought upon himself by his actions. Ah, Lady Ashington! How colourful you look, my dear, in that interesting dress! May I introduce Mrs Oscar Wilde?"

There is one more brief paragraph in my diary for that date:

Towards the end of the evening I was introduced to Arthur Humphreys, the manager of Hatchards Book Store. He asked me whether I am thinking of doing any more writing. He says he was very impressed with my work! He has read "There Was Once", and my contributions to "The Bairns' Annual" and the R.D.S.'s "Gazette" – which Mr Hatchard published, of course. He was altogether most charming and complimentary, if a little shy, and I like him, in spite of O.'s waspish comments.

That was less than a fortnight before you took out a year's lease, without telling me, on the cottage at Goring-on-Thames. I'd had plans – plans I had shared with you – for both of us to holiday in Florence in the autumn, so that we could enjoy that beautiful city together. You had told me you thought it a delightful idea. But Bosie, of course, intervened, and you sold Goring to me under the pretext of a commitment to spend more time with the boys, who had been moved from pillar to post that year – how grateful I was for obliging friends! As for Tite Street – you seemed to have lost all interest in either living in our family home or in finding another, so I'd had no option but to renew the lease.

28th of June 1893
Goring-on-Thames

Well, so much for our happy family holiday by the river! It will be Babbacombe all over again, won't it, only this time I shall not leave the boys with O. and B. They want to stay, needless to say. To them, it seems only natural that their father should ask Bosie to join us, and it is all great fun, and they clamour ever morning to be allowed to go out with them in the boat.

But I have made it quite clear to O. that I am not going to share my holiday with Bosie again, and that I am not going to leave my children in his care. I shall see if Vyvyan can go to Rottingdean, to stay with the Burne-Joneses. His health continues to be delicate, he is always coming down with something or other, and he has also become so wilful ... several friends have suggested to me that he just wants attention, but I have so much else on my mind at present that I find I am not the right person to give it to him. So if the Burne-Joneses can have him, it will be ideal for he will be in the bosom of a happy family while Cyril, who is much easier to manage, can stay with me. If not, it will have to be Dublin.

O. seemed rather taken aback by my firmness; he reminded me that I had issued a long-standing invitation to B., and had encouraged him to consider himself part of the family. I reminded <u>him</u> that this was over a year ago, and that a lot of water had flowed under the bridge since then.

He looked startled. "What do you mean by that?" he asked.

I did not wish to go into specifics; he already knows my opinion of him and Bosie greeting the local vicar half naked, and I told him of Miss Simmons' consternation at the Regatta when she spied him with an arm around the boy who looks after the boats (we are now in danger of losing a perfectly good governess after less than a month, not because of the boys' behaviour, but because of O's!) I contented myself with commenting that he must think me very stupid. This must have bothered him, for he said nothing at all, but smoked a cigarette and stared at me reproachfully.

This morning he said to me, before Bosie was down, "Constance, my dear, do you not think it will look rather odd, your leaving here so precipitately just after Bosie arrives?"

I was astonished. "Odd? You are afraid of looking odd? To whom, pray, do you wish to avoid giving this impression? Not the locals, surely – it's a little late for that, is it not?"

Oh, he has never seen me so spiteful and waspish. He actually stammered over his reply.

"Well, well, I mean ...well, what about our friends? Your friends, and mine?"

"Your friends?"

"Well, yours then. And our families. My mother. What are you going to tell them?"

So that was it. "I shall tell your mother the truth, of course," I answered smugly.

He responded to the word in much the same way as Pontius Pilate: "The truth, what is that?"

"Well, isn't Bosie here to work on his translation of "Salome"? He is obviously finding it impossible, with the boys here, for he's done no translating at all this past week. Our leaving will let you both work in peace."

His relief was palpable. "Oh, Constance ..." he said, and then added in a quiet voice "I wish you would like Bosie. I thought you did like him."

"No-one likes Bosie, Oscar. Not even his own father likes him, from what I hear."

He said first of all that this was a lie, and then, conceding that it was true, that the Marquess was mad, and that this was a fact known to the world at large, and that I must also be mad if I believed the kind of things he was saying. Of course I replied that I had no idea what kind of things he was saying, but that if they were the same kind of things as what he was reputedly saying about his eldest son and Lord Rosebery, then he and Bosie should have much more to worry about than what Speranza might think of my taking the children to Rottingdean.

For a moment – just one moment – I thought he was going to be honest with me, at last; but I suppose my angry demeanour forbade it. He merely said, "It would be helpful if you could stand by me, Constance."

Torn between concern for him on the one hand, and outrage on the other that he should have so little consideration for my feelings as to expect me to support him in his recklessness, I did not reply; and in any case, at that moment the door burst open and the children tumbled into the room, faces aglow with energy and enthusiasm, determined not to miss one minute of these last precious days with their Papa.

27th of March 1898
Nervi

It is strange to recall, with hindsight, how much I knew, and yet how little. For were you not being blackmailed on and off during most of that year, with your letters to Bosie passed back and forth between various unsavoury persons? And were you not at the same time, almost under my very nose, consorting with young boys supplied to you by Alfred Taylor, boys sometimes *no older than our sons are now*? Is it any wonder that when all this became public knowledge, during the trials, I refused to see you?

It would be helpful if you could stand by me, Constance – how dared you say that to me, Oscar, knowing as you must have done that I would think you referred only to your relationship with Bosie?

I told the whole story to Georgina, you know. I confided everything – my suspicions, my fears, my fury. She had guessed most of it long ago. I remember kneeling beside her chair, sobbing into her lap, drenching the old-fashioned silk skirt with my tears as she softly stroked my head. At length she raised my face, gently but firmly, and held my gaze with those dark eyes, so luminous beneath the white hair and the widow's cap.

"Constance," she said, "my dear, I know it is a

heavy burden, but it *would* be helpful if you could stand by him. A wife is her husband's conscience, never more so than when he has none of his own. Think of it as an illness – you would not desert him, would you, if he lay sick? You would do all in your power to make him well again. Let your faith be your guide – all is not lost, and remember, joy shall be in Heaven over one sinner that repenteth, more than over ninety-and-nine just persons, which need no repentance."

She calmed me, and I returned to Tite Street to shoulder my burden as best I could, with friends and family enquiring after you and praising my sensible decision to allow you peace and quiet to work. Oh, very dutiful and loving they must have thought me, and so I was content to be seen. I even wrote and published my last short story on precisely that theme – *The Little Swallow*.

You complimented me on it, of course. You thought the little heroine charming and tender-hearted, nursing the injured bird back to health and then having her heartbreak at its escape through the open window rewarded by its daily return to be fed. To you it was your mother all over again, earning your father's dying (or was it undying?) gratitude by allowing him the freedom to keep a mistress.

Qui Patitur Vincit – She Who Suffers, Wins. My letters to Georgina at that time were full of references to your "ill health", to my having recourse to daily prayers and visits to the Oratory to burn candles at the Virgin's altar. When you finally returned to London, having quarrelled so violently with Bosie that you'd begged his mother to send him abroad for a while, I thought that my prayers had been answered.

But if truth be told, in spite of my best efforts to convince myself otherwise I was done with playing the martyr. In *The Little Swallow* I was letting you know, Oscar, that your freedom came with conditions attached; and you did indeed come daily to Tite Street to be fed, whilst I allowed you your rooms at St James' Place.

2nd of January 1894

My thirty-sixth Birthday! Received beautiful bouquets this morning from O. and from Georgina. I am expecting O. to visit, but not until after lunch since he never rises earlier nowadays. At breakfast the boys presented me very solemnly with two little parcels which they had obviously wrapped themselves. Vyvyan's contained a pincushion of rose-coloured silk, heart-shaped and edged with lace, which he said was his own choice, and I can well believe it for Miss Simmons would never have chosen such a thing! Cyril, I think, had been less wayward and consulted her judgement – his parcel contained a beautiful pair of lilac-coloured silk gloves. It is always such a joy to receive presents from the children, for they are given so unselfconsciously, and with true love. I have promised to keep the pincushion by me always, and to wear the gloves immediately I next go out.

I wonder what my thirty-seventh year will bring? It has already begun in happier circumstances than last year's birthday, because Bosie stays away. I hear that he has been offered the post of honorary attaché to Lord Currie in Constantinople! That should keep him out of O.'s concerns for a while. It is strange, is it not, that Lady Q. should now be so keen to keep them apart, when she seemed to be actively encouraging their association last year. I know that O. has not told me the whole truth. He refuses to say much about it, but he is very definite that both he and Lady Q. wish Bosie to stay abroad.

He will not tell me the cause of their quarrel; he will only say that B. has a fearful temper, and that he keeps him from his work. I think he is becoming a little afraid of him, incredible though it seems – a man of O.'s calibre afraid of a boy not yet twenty-one! But at least he is recognising at last the extent of B.'s influence over him, and the unhealthy nature of that influence. How wonderful if my prayers were to be answered at last!

O. has not yet fully returned home. He still lodges at St James' Place, which could of course mean that he really is immersing himself in his work - or that he has got so used to living as a bachelor that he has no intention of returning to married life. Only time will tell.

But be that as it may, I am determined to enjoy the peaceable friendship that presently exists between us, including as it does regular trips to the theatre (just like the old days!), visits to friends who are delighted to welcome us as a couple once more, and the occasional honest conversation which gives me hope that we can find a way forward, after all.

Those four months, from October to February, were like a safe harbour after a storm. Everyone told me I had done well, that I was being a wonderful wife – Georgina complacent in seeing her advice bear fruit, your mother delighted to have us both frequent guests at Oakley Street once again – and although our marriage could never be what once it was, I thought that a small price to pay for a peaceable family life. After a while, lulled into a false sense of security, I even thought once again that there was no harm in allowing you the company of your charming young friends, that I could rise above the miasma of the commonplace just as your mother had done with your father. And it was this that led me, in a moment of madness, to make the worst mistake of all.

28th of February 1894

The most extraordinary thing has happened. I have received a telegram from Bosie. It really is addressed to me, and arrived here this morning. It is now late afternoon, and I have read it several times, and still do not know what to do about it.

  He wants me to speak to O. on his behalf, and ask him to agree to a meeting. He says that he must see him at least once, to make peace between them and to explain (he does not say what there is to explain). He says that even if O. will not accept him back as a friend, he wants at least to know that he does not hold him as an enemy. He says that O.'s friendship is the most precious thing he ever possessed in his life. He says that he knows O. holds me in the highest affection and respect, and will listen to me; and also that he has always had the greatest affection for me himself, and hopes that for the sake of the warm friendship that exists between us, I will use my influence to make peace between him and my husband. It is a very long telegram! I dread to think of the expense. But then expense has never been a matter of concern to Bosie.

Now, what am I to do? I know what I <u>should</u> do, if I have any pride. How dare that impertinent boy think to flatter me into acting as go-between! Any "warm friendship" which may have existed between us in the past is long dead, and he knows it. He merely wants to use me as an instrument of reconciliation between him and O. and once he has got what he wants, he will despise me once more. And O. will not thank me for it, in the long run. If they renew their friendship they will only continue as before – running up debts, behaving extravagantly without a care for what anyone may think; and O. will do no work, or anything he does write will be spoiled. I gather that B. made a terrible job of translating "Salome", and I suspect this to have been the cause of their quarrel. And what could I possibly have to gain from their reunion? Is it going to bring O. back home? Have things not been so much better between us lately, with B. away?

And yet, and yet ... Bosie's absence has <u>not</u> made O. come back to me; and it is possible they will both value me more, and respect me more, if I show myself to be understanding of their friendship.

But no, this is foolish. These are dreams of the past, and I am done with fooling mysef in that way. There is no room between them for me. No, I will not do it. I will send a brief, firm message making it quite clear that I do not interfere in my husband's affairs, for better or for worse; and I will say, while I am about it, that in my opinion this separation is very much for the better. There!

But I didn't, did I, Oscar? I never sent that brief, firm message. In a desperate effort to command your affection and gratitude, in a misguided act of trust that I hoped would place me once more at your side with him at our feet, I summoned you to Tite Street, showed you the telegram, and asked whether you thought his expressions of remorse and contrition were genuine.

It would be helpful if you could stand by me, Constance ... I wish you would like Bosie ... It was what you wanted, was it not? And you kissed me on the lips, and left for Paris the following day.

It was in the Spring of that year that the boys went away to school. I will never forget the sight of Cyril in his little blazer and tie, sitting forlornly upon his trunk in the hallway waiting for the carriage that was to take us to Haywards Heath. It took the greatest of efforts not to let him see my tears. I could not help asking myself, why are we doing this? I remembered my poor brother crying night after night before he was sent away to school, and my heart all but broke to think of our boys suffering likewise.

But Cyril didn't cry, at least not to my knowledge. He was just very pale and quiet, and would come to climb upon my knee, as he used to when a baby. And you, who should have been a support and comfort to us both, were not there. You had left the choice of our son's schooling, and the painful duty of preparation and separation, entirely to me.

I had chosen Bedales because it was a new, experimental sort of school that combined the usual curriculum of study with outdoor pursuits such as carpentry, land husbandry and gardening. It was in my mind that our son would come under a more masculine influence there than had been the case in recent years. And for Vyvyan, I chose Hildersham House in Broadstairs, where the estuary air would do him good and where the headmaster was reputed to be kind.

"If I don't like it, Mama, I may come home, mayn't I?" whispered Cyril, laying his face against my shoulder; and I lied, "Yes, of course, darling, but you must give it time. It is bound to feel unusual at first, and you must promise me to try to get used to school life, and to do your best to please the masters and learn your lessons."

Thankfully his friendly and easy-going nature helped him to settle in quickly, and finding himself both popular and successful, he never did beg to come home.

I took Vyvyan to Broadstairs the following week – he was the littlest boy at the school, and we could easily have waited a couple of years, until he also reached the age of nine – but if truth be told I was finding his crankiness and neediness so difficult, and money was tight once again, and by sending them both away I could dispense with the ever-critical Miss Simmons. I know many people thought it strange that I should separate the boys, but the regime at Bedales would never have suited Vyvyan. He missed Cyril at first, I think, more than he missed me; but he settled at Broadstairs in the end, and indeed became quite a favourite with both masters and boys.

Oh Oscar – I have judged you harshly for neglecting our boys, but I do know how deeply you love them. A couple of nights ago I re-read those letters you wrote to the *Daily Chronicle* – I kept the cuttings. I can still hardly bear to read about the poor children you encountered in prison. When I first read that letter last year, I cried for days. How you must have suffered, being such a tender father yourself, to witness the cruelties inflicted upon that poor little boy; to hear him crying again and again for his parents, to see the wardens, instead of comforting him, speak sternly and shut the door of his cold, dark cell. Oh, if I knew that such a thing were happening to one of our boys, I should tear down the door with my bare hands! I should go mad with the outrage of it. A system that convicts young children of crimes they can hardly understand, or have had intention to commit, cannot possibly be worthy of the term "Justice". How can we live in such a world?

Oscar, I now wish that I had let you see the boys when you first came out of prison. I know that you longed to see them, that it would have done your heart good to see them; and perhaps if you had, you would never have felt the need to go back to your old life, and to *him*. I was wrong, wasn't I? But everyone urged me to wait. They said it would be better to take things slowly. And now you have not even acknowledged the photographs I sent you; you have hardened your heart.

When I have had this operation, I shall have both of them to stay here at the Villa Elvira and you shall come to visit us, provided you come alone. I never meant to deny you your children, Oscar.

You once said – do you remember? - when Cyril was a baby, that every child should each day be hugged by his father and told that he was wonderful. I remembered that, when I sent them away to school. And you, Oscar – you were not even there to give them a hug goodbye. You were finally enjoying the delights of Florence, delights I had once hoped to revisit with you myself - with Bosie.

29th of March 1898
Nervi

Oh God, Oscar, I have had another terrible dream, this time about Cyril. It has upset me so much that I could not eat breakfast, and Maria has sent me back to bed; so I am sitting here supported upon the pillows, writing this in my own hand. See how illegible my writing has become! My hand moves so slowly, and aches after only a few strokes of the pen. It does not matter for this, as you will never read it, but I am in the middle of a letter to Vivian which I *must* finish, and now I want to write one to Cyril also, and one cannot type-write a letter to a child.

Maria knows that I slept badly, and thinks I am worried about my journey to Genoa next week, and the operation. Well, I must admit that I am, even though I have been under Dr Bossi's knife before; I am dogged by a sense of urgency, as though I were aiming to complete this long confession before I leave – which would in any case be impossible, as there is still so much to say, and only a few days left now. I tell myself I can easily complete it when I return, that it will enliven my convalescence, and give me a way to feel in touch with you – and you shall come here to visit me when I am feeling better. I suppose Carlos Blacker has told you about my operation? I should have written properly to tell you myself, I know. The Ranee says to me frequently, "Have you written to Oscar?" - and I answer truthfully, "I am writing ..." But she knows that no letter has been sent, and accuses me of prevaricating.

I may as well admit the truth, Oscar – I fear that I am going to die. I am sure it is that fear which is sending me these terrible nightmares.

Last night I dreamt that Cyril was trapped at the bottom of the overgrown gardens at Babbacombe, halfway down the cliff. I could see him lying on his face. He was quite a little boy again, about seven years old, just as he was when you and he made sandcastles on the beach in winter. I called his name, and tried to run down the cliff to him, but my feet became ensnared in the weeds, and Vivian was beside me, hanging on to my skirts and sobbing hysterically. I saw Cyril try to raise himself, to claw his way up towards me, but there was a red stain where his head had been lying, and I screamed as he turned his face towards me and I saw that half of it was gone, leaving a mess of blood and shattered bone. I tried to scream again, to wake myself, for I knew at some level that I was dreaming - and then, miraculously, I had reached him and lifted him in my arms, and the blood was gone from his face but it was the face of a little baby again. His round, blue eyes were filled with tears, the corners of his mouth turned down in that expression of disappointed reproach he used often to give us when we removed some forbidden object from his grasp – and as I surfaced to waking, I knew that my baby was dead.

This morning I fully expected to receive a telegram from Neuenheim saying that some dreadful accident has occurred – but none has arrived, thank God. I am trying to pull myself together; I am tempted to telegraph and ask for permission for Cyril to come and spend a few days here before I go to Genoa – I'm sure it would be granted, if I explain that I am to have a serious operation. But it would only alarm him, wouldn't it, and disrupt his studies; it would be selfish of me, just for the sake of having sight of him and trying to allay my own foolish fears. I shall have to content myself with writing him an especially loving letter, once I have finished writing to Vivian.

My hand is aching badly now; I had better rest it for a while. Tomorrow, I hope, I will be back at my typewriter.

2nd of May 1894

This morning I received an unexpected call from Mr and Mrs Arthur Humphreys! I had never met Mrs H. before – she is a very pleasant woman, but plain and quiet. I was surprised that they should come to see me knowing that O. was from home, but it transpires that Mr Humphreys has a literary proposition to put to me. He would like to publish a collection of O.'s most entertaining epigrams, and wonders if I would be interested in collaborating!

He wants me to make a personal selection. I thought at first that he was joking, but he really does appear to be serious - he seemed quite put out when I laughed! He says that the reading public would love a selection chosen by the person who knows O. most intimately. Had it not been for the presence of Mrs H., I would have been tempted to refer him to Bosie Douglas ...

What could I say? I could hardly tell him that nowadays I read most of O.'s witticisms in the newspaper, like everyone else. Even in the past, constant exposure to his well-rehearsed aphorisms made me a little less rapturous about them than I was supposed to be. When one has heard the same anecdote five or six times, one starts to wonder why one ever thought it witty in the first place ... I seldom gave in to the temptation to spoil it for him, and on the rare occasions when I did he would cold-shoulder me for the rest of the evening.

Of course I did not mention any of this to Mr Humphreys. I have agreed to consider his proposal, subject to O.'s approval; I am certainly not going to spend my time concocting a tribute that he does not want! I shall be interested to see what he thinks of the idea ...

14th of May 1894

Have been to see Mr Humphreys at his office, to tell him that we have O.'s approval for a selection of his epigrams. It is to be called "Oscariana". O. seems quite taken with the idea, though somewhat amused that Mr H. should have approached me instead of him. He says he only brought his wife along as a chaperone, such nonsense! Anyway, he does of course want to have full control of the rights but will leave the selection up to me. I am still not sure whether I am pleased to have been set such a task; but Mr Humphreys has such a naive enthusiasm about the idea that it is difficult to resist him. He is obviously a great admirer of O.'s, and was very sweet to me, and says he is sure we will work well together. There is something about him that reminds me of a little boy (a very tall little boy!) who has been promised a treat, and makes me feel it would be cruel to let him down, or disillusion him in any way. And after all, it will be nice to have something to do ... I find I am missing the children terribly.

I am thinking ahead to the summer holidays, and considering Miss Lord's offer of renting her little house at Worthing for the month of August for me and the boys, with or without O. I am going to try and engage the Swiss governess recommended by Aunt Mary, before she is snapped up by someone else. She is said to be very good with boys, and ours will probably need a firm hand after having been at school ...

30th of June 1894

Something really awful happened this afternoon, and I am still shaking with the shock of it. The Marquess of Queensberry has been here in the house, having the most dreadful row with O. in his study. I could hear it from the landing. He was demanding that O. discontinue his association with his son, and he said — I can hardly write it — he said it is <u>common knowledge</u> that I am planning to divorce him for unnatural behaviour! Common knowledge, what on earth can he mean? I have <u>never</u> said to <u>anyone</u> that I would even consider divorcing O. The shouting and the noise was terrible. Lady Q. was quite right, the man is insane.

O. has left the house and refuses to talk about it, although I actually tried physically to restrain him, and make him tell me what is going on. He is obviously shaken and upset, and promises that I shall have a full explanation "when he has sorted the matter out", whatever that means.

What am I to do? I have no-one to turn to except Georgina, who is already so worried about me, or Aunt Mary, who is already so judgemental about O. I could write to Otho, but I am loathe to put pen to paper for fear of who else might read it. Someone, it seems, has been spreading the most disgusting lies. I am too upset to write about it. I am going to take some brandy, and lie down.

How well I remember that horrible occasion! You had arrived for lunch, as was now and again your wont - it was so unfair on Cook, as you never let us know in advance – but of course I made you welcome, and if you seemed a little preoccupied I saw nothing unusual in it. I had been finding the June heat oppressive, and retired upstairs for a short rest. You promised to say goodbye before you left.

I must have drifted off to sleep, for I was jolted violently awake by the sound of shouting rising up the stairwell. Oh! I was sure we had been invaded by a gang of roughs! My heart was pounding as I rushed out onto the landing, but by the time I'd descended to the first floor, you were ushering the visitor into your study and closing the door. I heard you say, *"Someone has been telling you an absurd set of lies about your son and me!"* and I realised with a shock that this loud-mouthed intruder must be the Marquess of Queensberry, and that the events of which Lady Queensberry had forewarned me the previous year had finally come upon us.

I did not know, of course, that you had already met him several times and that there had been an angry exchange of letters between father and son. This was the first inkling I had, that you were in real danger from that man.

I could not hear all that followed; unless you were shouting, your voices were indistinct. But I certainly heard enough: *"It is all over London that your wife is petitioning to divorce you for your unnatural behaviour! If I catch you and my son together in public, I shall thrash you within an inch of your life!"*

"How dare you! What are you accusing me of, Lord Queensberry? What exactly are you accusing me of?"

There was more muffled remonstration, then he roared, *"I do not say you are it, Sir, but you look it!"* - and you both erupted into the hallway.

I saw him from the landing – a short, squat, brutish-looking man, his coarse features contorted with rage. I saw also, with a stab of fear, that he had not come unaccompanied, though the broad-shouldered rough he'd brought with him had presumably stayed silent throughout the interview. I realised how brave you had been in standing up to him, outnumbered two to one like that. I heard you say to the servants that this was the Marquess of Queensberry, and that they were never to allow him entrance to our house again.

We were both badly shaken, but you would not stay to discuss it. When I clung to your coat and cried that I was not planning to divorce you, how could you think it, but that I had to know what was going on, you put me gently aside. "I will tell you everything later, Constance," you said; "I am sorry you have had to witness this."

Then you left the house, and you never did tell me everything until it was far, far too late, and your public humiliation had become mine also.

The next day, desperate for some advice and comfort, I went to visit your mother at Oakley Street. The dear old thing was delighted to see me – I had been neglecting her of late, and felt ashamed. We drank tea in the drawing room – as always, the curtains were drawn, and at eleven o'clock in the morning, in the middle of June, she received me by candlelight. It gave me a sense of having been transported from my own time and space back into the past, to be sitting in the big old armchair with its fringed antimacassar, sipping tea in the company of an elderly lady whose rings chinked softly as she replaced her cup in its saucer and whose pale, wide brow reflected a waxy glow from the candles. The room smelt of stale air, and whisky.

We spoke of your brother Willie, and his recent re-marriage.

"Lily is a good girl, a very nice girl, Constance, I am sure you will like her. I admit that I had my doubts at first, but I am happy to have been proved wrong. She is not at all like the other one, and has given him her love, which I hope and pray may be his salvation. It breaks my heart, my dear, to see such open enmity between my sons; I had so hoped Oscar would put in an appearance at the wedding. If I were to invite you both to meet them, here under my roof, would he come, do you think?"

"I fear not," I replied gently. "He seems to have hardened his heart against Willie; he has never forgiven him for that lukewarm review of *Lady Windermere* he wrote for *Vanity Fair* ..." (I did not add that the real strain in your brotherly relations revolved around Willie's constant sponging for money, for I knew she would not want to hear it.)

"But Willie has a career to make also!" she protested; "Oscar has made his, and should not begrudge his brother!"

"I know, Mama; I know."

"Will you at least try to persuade him, Constance?"

"I will try, but I would not want to raise your hopes. Really, I see so little of Oscar nowadays, and my powers of persuasion are not at all what they were. But I will meet them myself, with pleasure."

"If this enmity continues to my grave it will break my heart. I never thought my sons would break my heart. First my husband, then my little girl, now Oscar and Willie, who are all I have to live for. How many times can a woman's heart be broken, do you think? Too many times, I fear."

She rose, and made for the decanter upon the sideboard. I was only surprised that she had held out for so long. A wave of pity swept over me. Could she, the ardent young girl who had penned such stirring ballads all those years ago, have foreseen herself now, at seventy, what would she have thought? Her magnificence derided as obsolescence, her genius faded into mediocrity, her passionate hopes into compromise – how she would have wept. But along the way, she had been someone in her own right.

I smiled and shook my head as she gestured with the decanter towards me. She came and sat down again opposite me; the light caught the rim of the glass she was holding.

"And how is *your* heart, Constance? Ah, my dear, do not turn your face away. You have been unhappy, I can see it. Why is my son so neglectful of his wife? Tell me frankly, Constance, have there been harsh words between you? Do you suspect him of having done you wrong?"

What could I say? I longed for advice, for comfort, but she knew nothing. She feared, Oscar, that you would break her heart, but she little suspected how violent the blow would be when it came. She inquired, querulously, about your neglect of me – was it your work? Your public engagements? Did I suspect an attachment to another woman? She could assure me she had heard nothing of the kind herself, but a wife could always tell. If there were a woman in the case, my heart would inform me quicker than any gossip.

I reassured her that we'd had no quarrel; that I had no reason to believe there had ever been another woman; that you were working on a new play, and that I felt lonely and a little sorry for myself, the children being from home. I told her also, in case such rumours as Lord Queensberry had spoken of should ever reach her, that I would always stand by you. She kissed me, and spoke of her great affection for me as a daughter-in-law, her delight in her grandchildren whom she longed to see when they returned from school, and her hopes that Willie and his new wife would be blessed with a daughter.

As I left, I told her we were planning a lovely family holiday in Worthing, which I was sure would do us a world of good.

How could I have known that within a year the blow would have fallen, and shattered her poor old heart? That within two years she would be dead? And I, in exile, unable to be with her at the end, to hold her hand and speak of you, to say that I was sorry for deceiving her and ask for forgiveness.

When I visited her after your imprisonment (I made only one visit, before I came abroad), she clasped my hand in hers and asked just one question: "Constance, did you know?"

I told her that I had known.

"All along?"

"Yes, Mama," I whispered, lowering my eyes, unable to hold her steady gaze. "All along."

Her hand, withered and heavy with rings, withdrew from mine.

"If you had told me," she said reproachfully, "I would never have urged him to stay and stand trial. I believed he was innocent. I told him that only a guilty man would run away. You should have told me." She wept for sorrow, and I wept for shame.

At least she lived to hold Willie's little girl in her arms.

When I returned home from Oakley Street, dazed and ill at ease in the June sunlight, I found a card waiting for me: "Mrs Ernest Leverson" had called in my absence. Immediately my suspicions were aroused; she had come, I was sure, to discuss the rumours of divorce; to urge me to stand by you and support you; to tell me how fortunate I was in being your wife, how glad she would have been to have such a husband, how the intellectual satisfaction of being allied to such a genius must outweigh any compromises I must make in our marriage, and other things of that sort. So angry was I at the thought of being prescribed my duties by that particular woman that I committed a grave breach of social etiquette – I tore up her card, and did not return her call.

Her also I was to see once more in the throes of your humiliation, and that was when I came to visit you at her house, where you hid whilst awaiting a date for the second trial; when I urged you, bullied you, implored you to flee the country - I will not remind you or myself of what I said on that dreadful occasion. I ran down the stairs in tears, and Ada Leverson was waiting in the hallway, holding out her hand to me as I tried to brush past her.

"He will not listen to me!" I sobbed, too upset for dignity or pride. "He will not go. Is it you? Do you suport him in this madness?"

"Most certainly I do *not*, Constance," she replied emphatically. "Nobody wants him to stay, excepting Lady Wilde and Bosie. All the arrangements have been made: a boat is waiting, there is money ready. But he is set upon vindication, or martyrdom – nothing in between will do. I thought perhaps you could have swayed him ..."

"I?" I cried bitterly, "Why should *I* have any influence? *You* knew better than I what was going on. You warned me once about Bosie, but you yourself did nothing. You have watched all this unfold for your own amusement, as if it were one of his plays; but it is not *your* life that will now be ruined."

I never saw her again, so I do not know whether she told you of my outburst. No doubt she allies herself with those who advised you against coming back to me; if she does, I suppose it is my fault, for

I courted her enmity as assiduously as she courted your friendship.

There was one woman whose advice I sought in the end that summer, and that was Mrs Robinson, your "Sybil". I consulted her before we went to Worthing. The dimness of her little parlour, heavy with velvet swags and with the smell of incense, was reminiscent of your mother's drawing room, and I felt a momentary pang of guilt in confiding to a stranger what I had failed to reveal to my own mother-in-law. But of course, this wily old Sybil knew you well, and Bosie too.

"I see a new choice before you," she said to me. "A choice between duty and love. The love is a forbidden love, and the duty a thankless duty; but whichever you choose, my dear, your name will forever be linked with your husband's. He is treading a dangerous path, and yours is not the same path, but it will always run parallel. Choose wisely."

What did she mean by that, Oscar? Everything and nothing. Do you know, to this day I cannot decide whether your Mrs Robinson was a clever charlaton or a genuine but fallible seer. She failed you, didn't she? She prophesied triumph, and encouraged you in your recklessness, and gave you false confidence in treading your dangerous path.

And to me, she said: "Your name, your husband's name, is a name that will be remembered."

How cruelly that now rings true! And I have changed my name, and our children's, in the hope that we will not be remembered alongside you; but I have not divorced you, as so many urged me to do; I never could bring myself to finalise our separation in that way. I know it is not the same as standing by you, as I promised your mother I would, but it is something.

As for the "forbidden love" - well, I naturally assumed that she referred to you and Bosie. How little I anticipated what lay around the corner of my own heart!

1st of April 1898
Villa Elvira
Nervi

Well, Oscar, I am almost packed and ready to leave. I go to Genoa tomorrow. The Ranee has offered to accompany me, and Carrie Blacker to meet me there, but I have refused them both – I would much rather go alone, and look forward to seeing my friends afterwards, when I am well set on the journey back to health.

I have prepared a postcard for Otho, who has shown much concern about me like the good brother he is, and will have Maria send it from Genoa. I am hoping he will come to collect me from the nursing home when it is all over. He and Mary have been so good to me and the boys, welcoming us into their home when we could not find accommodation elsewhere and doing all they could for us; and I hope you have not forgotten, Oscar, how he visited you in prison to bring you news of us. He visits me often, and the locals here know that he is my brother and have nothing but praise for him.

I have also written to both the boys - I have mentioned you in my letter to Vivian, Oscar, and though I still could not bring myself to tell him exactly what happened to you, I have couched it in a way which I hope he will understand when he is older: I reminded him that you are his father and that you love him, and told him that all your troubles arose from a son's hatred for his father, and that I want him to keep on loving you no matter what. Just in case something should happen to me.

No. I must not talk like that.

And now, what am I to do with all this? I mean this letter, and the diaries? Last night I dreamt that I burned them ... but I want to continue when I come back, so I must find a safe place to stow it all away. I cannot send you what I've written, because you would need the diaries also, and I cannot send those through the post; as it stands it would be incoherent, and moreoever it is unfinished, so what would be the point of sending it? And I have not yet told you the most important thing. About Arthur.

Oh, perhaps I *should* burn everything, just in case ... I would not want anyone but you to read this ... it is not very pleasant to think that all one's friends, not to mention one's enemies, will find out the truth about one's character after one's death ...

But I will feel very silly when I come back well and fit and ready to pick up the threads again, if I have burned all these interesting documents in a fit of morbid despair. I shall put them safely away in my trunk, and go and rest as Maria advises me to do, before I finish packing. I am taking my Keats with me, of course, to console me during my period of recovery; also my rosary beads. I have taken to saying a few Hail Marys morning and evening ... I

find God's Mother easier to approach than God
Himself these days …

I have not told Georgina about this operation,
Oscar. She does not believe Dr Bossi has done me
any good in the past, and she would not approve of
my putting myself once more in his hands. She
does not think that "women's problems" are the
source of my discomfort at all. But she is not here
to advise and help me, unlike the Ranee and Carrie
Blacker; and shallow creature that I am, there is a
part of me that resents her absence and feels
neglected, even though I know she is frail, and unfit
to travel. So at precisely the time when I am most
in need of a Mother's comforting presence and
advice, my spiritual Mother must remain in
ignorance. I hope she will forgive me, and that we
will be able to meet in person this Summer – it
seems so long since I've enjoyed her soothing
presence. She sheltered me, you know, during that
awful time when your first trial broke down and the
second, with its foregone conclusion, loomed over
us like a stormcloud. From my visit to you at the
Leversons', I fled straight to her. And she took me
in, despite opposition from her friends and family,
as did the Napiers.

Aunt Mary – I have not told her either, bless her,
for I have worried her enough these past three years.
It was to her house that I fled in the first instance,
following your arrest, it was with her help that I
made arrangements for the boys to be sent over to
Ireland, and then on to Switzerland with Mlle
Schuwer. It was she who first helped me to plan for
the worst, and enlisted the help of the Burne-

Joneses, and Sir George Lewis, and I don't know who else, to sort out my legal position following our separation.

Oh, I have been so blessed in my family and friends. Why have I never appreciated them as I ought? Why did I never appreciated the happiness on offer to me, just because it did not come from you? Why did I never divorce you? Why did I send Arthur away?

…......

The curtain is moving in the breeze … it comforts me, like the rocking of a cradle. Green, with turquoise motif – what are they? Flowers? Dragons? I always loved green. These are decadent curtains; you would not find them in an English hospital. The colours absorb the pain a little, and I find some ease.

Well, it is over; and the nuns who nurse me are kind, and bring me morphine for the pain, and do everything for my comfort. They have laid me on my side today, and I cannot move without help, so I watch the light move slowly across the window, and the curtain stirring where they have opened it a little to let in fresh air. Faint voices drift up from the grounds below; a bell tolls in the distance. I remind myself that you, Oscar, suffered worse things in prison.

If I could go back – oh, a long way back in my life, I could make all things as new as this new morning. This must be what a newborn baby sees, light and movement, the edge of a curtain dancing in the breeze. And all sound is muffled.

I have short, jagged periods of sleep, and when I wake the bedclothes are drenched in sweat. In my dreams I hear people shouting, aiming words at me like sharp, black beads.   What are they saying? Next time I awake, I will try to make sense of it. Is it just my name that I hear, repeated over and over? *Constance! Constance! Constance!*

....

You called my name, and I ran out of the house, out of the front door and across the street to the beach; there were carriages, and pedestrians on the street turning to stare, and families on the beach. This was Worthing, not Babbacombe; there were no nooks and crannies in which to hide.

I walked along the Esplanade, wringing my hands. My agitation drew curious glances, but I kept my head down and walked to the pier, and to the end of the pier, and then all the way back to the house. You were there in the little front parlour, alone. I tried to dash past, to go up to my room, but you ran out and caught me by the arm.

"Constance."

"Let me go, Oscar."

"Constance, I have got to talk to you."

"I don't want to talk. Leave me alone."

"Constance *please.*   Come in here, *please*, the children will hear. Just one brief word, I beg of you."

I followed you into the room, and you closed the door. Wearily I sat down upon the sofa.

"Where are they?"

"Gone."

"Gone where?"

"Away. Does it matter? Constance, please listen. I

am sorry that you saw what you did. I am sorry that I allowed Bosie to bring him here. It will not happen again, my dear; please try to put it out of your mind."

"What will not happen again, Oscar?"

"Well, this – this intrusion into your domestic life. I have told Bosie he is not to bring any more of his - friends to this house. Really, the last thing I want to do is to upset you, Constance. I promise to be more careful ..."

"More careful? Careful to keep your sordid life out of sight, is that what you mean? You do realise, don't you, that *our children could have walked past that door at any moment*?"

"No! I mean yes, I suppose that is what I mean, and no, I made sure the boys were out with Fräulein Zeigler, or I would never ..."

"I see. May I go now?"

"Constance, please try to understand."

"Oh, I understand perfectly well, Oscar. You are not sorry for what you and Bosie are doing, but you are sorry that I saw you do it. You will not promise to give up your unsavoury companions and activities, but you will try to keep them out of my way. Oscar, I don't know exactly what age that young man was, but he cannot have been more than fifteen at most. Have you absolutely no sense of responsibility? In a few years' time your own sons will be that age – does that not even give you pause for thought?"

You sighed, a long, shuddering sigh, and held your head in your hands. At last you said quietly: "But you *knew*, Constance."

"I knew about you and Bosie, but not about *this*. Where do you meet these boys, Oscar? Do you do this in London? Of course you do, how stupid of me. You introduced me to that boy Edward Shelley, when I came home unexpectedly and found him in the house. How can you – how *can* you corrupt the young like this, when you have children of your own?"

You blushed deeply, and murmured something inaudible.

"What?" I asked sharply, "What did you say?"

"I do not corrupt them, Constance. There are boys that I know, but they are already hardened little … they are already leading that life, Constance, it is how they earn a living."

"Oh, I see. So you are kindly providing employment for the poor."

"I did not say that, Constance."

"Where do you meet them? On the streets?"

"My dear, you don't want to know all this."

"But I do! I do! I have a right to know, I demand to know. Where do you meet them? Do you bring them to our house on a regular basis, when I am away?"

"No! I have a friend called Alfred Taylor. He lives in Little College Street. He – arranges introductions. We go out for meals, to hotels … there. That is all. Now you know. What are you going to do, Constance? Are you going to divorce me, and take the boys away?"

You sounded so hopeless, so desolate, that I raged inwardly at my inability to keep pity at bay.

"No, of course not. What would I have to gain by

dragging our children's name in the mud?"

"Your freedom, my dear. A new husband, perhaps."

I was furious at having the tables turned on me at a time like this.

"What? It is you who want freedom, not I! Well, you have it. You have always taken it, anyway. Consider yourself free to do as you wish. And I do not want a new husband."

That was true. I would have given anything, there and then, to have my old husband back, the husband I had courted so shyly and married so proudly only a decade ago. Not this debauched and lascivious stranger.

"Constance, I know that Arthur Humphreys is in love with you."

"Don't talk nonsense, he's a married man," I said, and left the room.

I lay on my bed and sobbed until I was nearly sick. I remembered with revulsion my romantic indulgence of your friendships, and the spell cast over me, in the early days, by Bosie. I bit my nails to the quick, and damned him to Hell a thousand times. I thought of Ada Leverson, that wily old Sphinx on her pedestal; she knew you for what you were and revelled in it, and by watching you as I had done I felt that I'd brought myself down to her level. As for you, Oscar – well, I planned my revenge in this way and that, and swore that I would make you suffer.

When I came to myself, I found that you'd left for Brighton; and there was still the blood on my lips of all those words left unsaid, crying out for vengeance.

The boys had been clamouring to go out. They wanted to know where Bosie was – he'd arrived out of the blue as was his wont, apparently completely oblivious to his father's threats and determined to muscle in on our family holiday, as always. They wanted to go to the beach with you both, but I had no idea where you were so I sent them on a sedate afternoon walk with Fräulein Zeigler. Poor dears, this was not turning out to be a happy holiday for them; they were restless and demanding, estranged by school and unable to settle.

When you came in to find the parlour empty, you must have assumed I'd gone with them; but I was in the kitchen, checking the supplies, suspecting that the local cook we'd engaged was not above a little domestic pilfering. I found nothing amiss however, and after a while I made my way upstairs to lie down; as I passed the open door of the room I'd reluctantly allotted to Bosie, I saw you.

You were kneeling before a young boy lying on the bed, leaning over him, your fingers twined in his hair. With your free hand you were loosening his clothes, quickly, deftly, while Bosie sat poised on the edge of the bedside chair, watching with a greedy, hateful expression on his face. The boy slid his arm around your neck, and pulled you down to him. You kissed first his lips and then his throat, moving slowly down his body.

I should have backed away, quickly and silently, but I stood in the doorway for some time and watched you quite calmly, until Bosie looked up and saw me. I have never seen anyone's eyes become quite so round with shock. I turned and ran back down the stairs, along the passage to the front door, and out into the street. I heard your voices calling me: *"Constance! Constance! Constance!"*

……....

It is evening now. The English nurse brings a lamp, and shadows shoot out across the ceiling. She sets it down upon the corner table and looks towards me, hesitantly. I manage a smile.

"My dear. Are you awake? That was a good long sleep you had. How are you feeling now?"

"It hurts," I say. "It still hurts."

She places a cool hand upon my brow. "I will bring you something for the pain, then. But first the doctor would like to see you. Are you hungry now? Could you manage to drink some soup, do you think?"

"No, no, not yet." I shudder, feeling the nausea rise within me.

"I would like you at least to take some tea, Mrs Holland. You have had only water now for two days. You must have nourishment, or you won't be able to build up your strength, will you?"

"No, no ..."

But she calls one of the nuns, and they lift me and prop pillows at my head, and hold a cup to my lips. I manage a few sips, to please them; then abruptly, I begin to heave …

The doctor comes to examine me. He is not Dr Bossi; he is young, and quietly spoken. I am lying in fresh sheets now, turned onto my back, my upper body supported by pillows. I am sweating profusely; the pain as they lifted and turned me was excruciating. The doctor shows concern. He speaks to me slowly – he is perhaps unaware that my Italian is fluent. To the nurse he says quietly, *"Comincia a preoccuparmi – non va bene per niente."*

The kind nun bathes my face with a sponge. I stare at the lamp over in the corner, which blurs and dazzles like the sun. I think of Icarus, the wings melting on his back as he falls.

At last, they bring me morphine.

....

Yes, that was the Summer that changed everything. That was the sharp edge of my life. In less than a year, you would be in prison – how could I have known that? After you left for Brighton, I wrote to Arthur Humphreys. I called him "My own darling Arthur". I invited him to come to me.

We had been corresponding ever since I left London. We pretended that we had some unfinished business to discuss concerning *Oscariana*, but this was just an excuse; production of the book was largely in your hands now. You were unhappy with my selection, as I knew you would be, and determined to write a new set of aphorisms to bulk them out.

During June and July, however, we'd been meeting regularly at Arthur's office. We had decided to dispense with formality and use our Christian names before the incident at Tite Street with Lord Queensberry; but it was a couple of weeks after that horrible occasion, as I remember, that he first took my coat himself, and sent his clerk to lunch.

"Constance," he said, "You are unhappy. What is the matter?"

"Oh … it is nothing." I forced a laugh. "Oscar has been telling me about his new play. Do you know what it is to be called?"

"No, tell me."

"*An Ideal Husband.*"

He was silent. We exchanged a long, serious look. At last he said, "You find that ironic."

"Yes."

He seated himself opposite me, drew his chair up to the desk.

"Constance, I have no wish, no right to pry. But you seem so bleak; has something happened? Is there some new quarrel between you and Oscar?"

I opened my mouth to tell him, but no words came. How could I possibly explain? *It is all over London that your wife is petitioning to divorce you …* No. It could only make things worse.

"No – no," I said at last, "There is no quarrel between us. At least, no quarrel that has not been there for some time."

I saw the anxiety deepen in his always anxious eyes. He was nervous and concerned, and suddenly I loved him for it.

"I should never have burdened you," he said quietly, "with *Oscariana*. I didn't know, you see, that you were unhappy as Oscar's wife. I thought that the work would be a pleasure to you. Now I see that I may unwittingly have caused you pain. I am so sorry."

"Don't be," I said, and the tears brimmed even as I smiled. "It has been such a pleasure to work with you, and has made me forget my troubles for a while."

"Has it? Has it really?" He brightened, and clasped his long white hands together. "Even though we disagree on politics and social reform?"

"Oh, *that*." I pulled myself together, managed a smile, tried to steer the conversation into safer, shallower waters. "No, really, I am sorry to have been so vehement on the subject. But I do truly believe that social reform is both just and necessary, and I cannot pretend otherwise."

"I would not expect you to! A little healthy argument is good, don't you think, if one is to reach a balanced view? And I'll admit that you do have a point ..."

"I made several good points!"

"Well, one or two maybe.."

"I used to be much involved in politics, you know, years ago."

"I do know. You were a supporter of the late Lady Sandhurst."

"A supporter, and a close friend."

"She was a remarkable woman, by all acounts."

"She was. She would have flattened all your Conservative arguments with no trouble at all!"

"Would she, now?"

"You should have heard her speaking to the Women's Liberal Federation on Irish Home Rule!"

"Oh, dear ..."

"Or better still, on women's suffrage!"

"Now, if all women were as educated and

thoughtful as you, Constance, I might come round to the idea."

"Mr Humphreys, I do not believe you."

"No, I mean it. An intelligent woman *should* have a say in her country's future. But my own domestic experience teaches me that there are women on whom such an opportunity would be utterly wasted."

I shook my head warningly. I had vowed to myself that I would not allow him to speak ill of his wife. Aloud I said, "Well, one could say that of some men!"

"Oh." He assumed a chastened expression which made me laugh.

"Arthur, you know I did not mean you."

"Even though I am a Conservative?"

"Even though."

"Well, at least I have made you smile. That is one point in my favour."

He began to shuffle the papers about on his desk. My eye lighted upon a copy of *Today*, folded back at a certain page.

"Oh, no!" I laughed. He followed my gaze.

"Ah! Oh, yes. *Mrs Oscar Wilde At Home*. A most delighful feature, and my compliments to the editor."

I blushed. "It is only a shallow piece. They approached me, and ... well, one has to keep up appearances."

"No, really, it makes delightful reading."

"What, to hear about my tastes in embroidery and flower arranging?"

"Well, at least they did not ask for your views on

social reform!"

We laughed. I held out my hand for the offending newspaper, and our fingers brushed as he handed it to me.

"It came out a few days ago. Your deliveries must run somewhat late."

"Nothing of the sort. I just wanted to keep it by me, since I cannot have you by me as often as I would wish."

We stopped laughing. Suddenly he reached out and took my hand; it was unexpected, and I was too much taken by surprise to make the requisite attempt at withdrawal.

"Constance, believe me, I would do anything to make you happy. Oscar must be mad not to love you. I can't think what is the matter with him."

His innocence sobered me.

"You mustn't worry about me, Arthur. You mustn't feel sorry for me. I may not be such a pleasant person as you think me."

"Nonsense!" he replied, with such warmth and feeling that I felt all my resistance melting. I closed my eyes and felt the tears squeeze out onto my cheek.

"No, it is true, Arthur. Please let me go. You are a good person, a wonderful husband, and I am doing you a great wrong in letting you behave like this. I would not like to think … that your wife felt as wronged by you as I do by Oscar."

He gave a deep groan, and released my hand. I reached quickly for my handkerchief, and tried to compose myself. When I was able to look at him, I saw his pale eyes sad in his pale face, his straw-coloured hair tousled over his brow. He looked lost and bewildered. My heart lurched for him.

At last he said: "Oh, my dear, if only … my wife sees me as a very dull fellow, I'm afraid. One cannot, surely, feel so badly betrayed by a dull fellow like myself as by such a lord of language as Oscar."

I smiled sadly. "I would have thought it the other way around. I have no taste any more for the decadent life. You call yourself a dull fellow; I call you an ideal husband. Your wife is a very lucky woman, Arthur, and I hope and pray that she may long remain so."

I left him then. It was very difficult, like tearing away a layer of skin.

We met twice more, I think, before I left for Worthing; and each time I felt my resolve weakening, but managed to stand firm, and keep my promise to your mother. But then, when you and Bosie ran away to Brighton, I wrote to him and he came to me. Oh, the joy of being desired again, and of being loved with passion! He asked me, as he stroked my hair, as he kissed my neck, what had changed my mind, what had made me decide to love him after all, to what did he owe such great happiness?

And I told him. I told him everything.

………

The edge of the curtain is razor-sharp, like the edge between – oh, what? - one breath and another.

Breathe in, stop; breathe out. There is the edge. Between thinking and saying. Bite the tongue.

I am glad I burned those diaries. What was I thinking of? There is no such thing as the truth about me.

There is the starched uniform of the nurse. She must be very tall. She reminds me of someone … when I was little, when I was loved … someone with starched clothes, who rustled as she moved. Mama Mary.

………

Oh, Mama Mary! She was so kind to me, she was my first Mother. Before Margaret, before Georgina. I had another mother, of course, but she never loved me. Never. I loved staying at Mama Mary's house, in Dublin. She used to read me stories, and sit by me till I slept. And when I was older, she gave such lovely parties for Otho and me. It was at one of her parties that I first met you, Oscar, do you remember?

You came with your brother. At first, I did not realise who you were – they were so many people, so many young men - but I was drawn to you at once. You wore a lily in your lapel, and your hair was like a lion's mane - clearly a follower of the Aesthetic Movement, someone with courage to rise above the petty conventions which so vexed my own restless spirit. You favoured me with a hesitant smile, and it touched me like a sudden rainbow. I thought, *"This man is less confident than he seems; he does not expect people to understand him."*

When I found out who you were, when I realised that I'd been engaged in private conversation with Oscar Wilde, aesthete *par excellence* and poet of the new age, I was so nervous in retrospect, and annoyed with myself for being nervous - but still desperate to see you again. When you sent that note inviting me to one of your mother's salons, I literally shook with fright …

But as time went by, and we met more and more frequently, I realised that with me you could drop the affectations you felt obliged to adopt as part of your public pose. I felt so privileged, so proud. It did not at first occur to me that I was falling in love; and when it did, I was sad, for the whole world knew you had eyes for no woman but Mrs Langtry.

You took me to the theatre to see Miss Terry in *Othello*, and I had to pretend to my family that the invitation came from your mother because they were so horrified; and then you went away to tour America, and I tried to forget you. But you came back, famous and successful, and we took up where we had left off. You took to calling me "Constance", not only in private but in conversation with other people, which scandalised the family still further … and then, of course, we got to the point where you kissed me for the first time - and I was a garden, a garden in bloom, a garden filled with white roses.

When Arthur kissed me, in that little house in Worthing, that whole garden blossomed again ...

. . . .

"Mrs Holland!"

The words fall from a great height. Who is that, what are they saying, who is Mrs Holland?

"Mrs Holland, my dear, don't cry. The doctor is here to see you. What is the matter? Is it the pain? Look, let us try to lift you. Your pillows are all awry."

Long arms reach down and I am pulled and jerked. It hurts, my skin is on fire, my tongue and throat are parched, my joints are melting. I try to speak, but my tongue is gone.

"Oscar," I try to say; the nurse strokes my head. She does not know who I am. She thinks I am a widow.

"I must see Oscar," I try again. "Please. Send for him."

"We have sent for your brother already, Mrs Holland. He will be here as soon as he can."

She thinks I have been calling for Otho.

. . . .

And his Soul said to him: "If indeed thou must drive me from thee, send me not forth without a heart. This world is cruel, give me thy heart to take with me." He tossed his head and smiled. "With what should I love my love, if I gave thee my heart?" he said.

He kissed me again, Arthur, in the empty hallway at Tite Street. The boys had returned to school, you had returned to Worthing to finish *The Importance*

Of Being Earnest, and I had returned to London to find myself faced with a situation for which I was not in the least prepared. A new novel, *The Green Carnation*, featuring Bosie and yourself grotesquely caricatured as "Lord Reggie Hastings" and "Esme Amarinth" was informing the reading public, with the barest veneer of subtlety, that you not only indulged in unnatural vice but also displayed an unhealthy interest in very young men. I was horrified.

By November, the caricatures were everywhere. *Punch* depicted you both as "a couple of Guys" awaiting the bonfire, wearing cauliflowers in your lapels: "Sir Fustian Flitters and Lord Raggie Tattersall await their youthful disciples," ran the caption. Even as *An Ideal Husband* went into rehearsal, preparing for its debut performance at The Haymarket, the rumour-mongers were doing their work and it was impossible to ignore them.

I told Arthur that I could not stay in London; I was going away, to Georgina at Babbacombe. He took both my hands in his own and spoke urgently, holding my gaze.

"It is not you who should be running away, my love," he said. "*You* have done nothing wrong. Divorce him. It is the only way. Then, if I can find a way – if I can persuade my wife to divorce me also -"

"Citing me as co-respondent?" I leapt backwards, snatching my hands back from his as though from a fire. He begged and pleaded.

"But we have to be brave, Constance! No-one, *no-one* will blame you, with such a husband. Our scandal will be as nothing to his. We can marry, and go to live abroad -"

"On what? And how, with my boys still at school in England? *What about them?* How will they live with such a double betrayal?"

"Constance, *please.* No-one will blame them, either. We will find schools for them on the Continent. They will have to change their name in any case; the name of Wilde will be tainted forever."

"No, Arthur. No!"

I thought of Cyril and Vyvyan, I thought of my promise to Speranza, I thought of you, abandoned to disgrace and ruin.

"I can't, Arthur," I said, and my voice, though breaking, was low and firm. "I cannot do this. I will not. Whatever happens, it will not be by my hand, not by my volition. I could never forgive myself."

He trembled, and his face was deathly pale. "It's all right, my love," he said, almost as though talking to himself. "You need not do anything. I know what to do."

…......

The young doctor comes to see me. He knows who I am. He speaks slowly and clearly, in Italian.

"Mrs Holland, the nurse tells me you have been asking for your husband. But your brother will be here very soon, and I really think it would be better if he sent for him. I do not see how we would go about contacting him directly – do you understand? Please try to be patient. Once Mr Holland Lloyd is here, he will be able to make any arrangements you wish for you to see your family."

I am feeling much better, in an odd sort of way; my whole body feels curiously light, as though I am hovering an inch or so above the bed.

"I want to see my children," I say, and my voice sounds as though it is coming from far, far away. "I miss my little boys." He pats my hand. His eyes are hooded with worry.

"Of course you do," he says. "Of course you do."

I realise that I am crying. Tears stream down either side of my face.

"I have not made proper arrangements," I try to say. "I do want them to see their father, I do. How will they ever see him again, if I die?"

"You mustn't talk like that, Mrs Holland. Your brother will be here very soon now. Do try and get some sleep."

He pats, not my hand again, but the little rosary clasped in my fingers. He goes, and I try to count the beads, but I cannot keep a grasp of them.

"Hail Mary," I whisper, "full of grace. Now and at the hour of our death, Amen." I cannot be bothered with the bit in between.

…......

We used to talk of my going on the stage, didn't we, Oscar? But I was never a successful actress until those last few months.

I was surprised at how easy it was, in the end, to stop seeing Arthur. Following the failure of your libel suit against Lord Queensberry, who had played his trump card to maximum effect, he pleaded with me one last time. He told me that Queensberry was planning to counter-sue. He said that his own contacts in the Conservative Party would be helping him; that they'd unearthed enough evidence to send you to prison, and had passed it all to Lord Queensberry's counsel. He said I must start divorce proceedings immediately, and distance myself and the boys from you as fast and as far as possible.

I ignored all his messages, and although I knew it was too little, far too late, I threw myself with every ounce of energy I possessed behind the husband I still loved and the rival I still loathed. When *The Importance of Being Earnest* opened at the St James, I arrived at the threatre decked out in white fur, with you on one arm and Bosie on the other. "If I have no concerns over my husband's friendship with this young man," I was saying to the world, "then why should you? It is harmless affection, nothing more. It is fashion, it is *la belle décadence,* it is play-acting. Think nothing of it – *I* don't!"

But the damage had been done.

....

Some kill their love when they are young,
And some when they are old.
Some strangle with the hands of Lust,
Some with the hands of Gold.
The kindest use a knife, because
The dead so soon grow cold.

I am cold now, Oscar. So cold, and yet so peaceful.
I can see myself from above, lying there on the bed.
I can see poor Otho on his way to Genoa, hurrying,

hurrying …

… and I see you, Oscar, much later, coming with red roses. Why red? It is white flowers that whisper of the garden - have you forgotten?

Still, they are beautiful. I'm glad we have forgiven one another. I shall be here waiting, Oscar, when you come. I shall greet you with a kiss.

……...

Constance died on 7th April 1898, and was buried in
Genoa. Her inscription described her simply as
Constance Mary, daughter of Horace Lloyd QC.
It was not until 1963 that her brother Otho's descendents
added the information *WIFE OF OSCAR WILDE.*

Oscar visited her grave just once, in February 1899. He
scattered red roses, and wept.
He died himself less than a year later, on 30th November
1900. He was buried at Bagneux; his remains were later
re-interred at the Père Lachaise cemetery in Paris.

Cyril and Vivian returned to England in the summer of
1898, where they were brought up by Aunt Mary Napier.
Cyril was killed during the First World War, at the
Battle of Festubert in May 1915.
Vyvyan reverted to the original spelling of his Christian
name, but kept the surname Holland. He married twice,
and had one son. In 1954 he published his
autobiography, *Son of Oscar Wilde.* He died in 1967.

Bosie Douglas married a female friend just two years
after Oscar's death. His life was never free from
controversy, and he was involved in several further libel
trials, either as plaintiff or as defendant. He died in 1945
in Lancing, East Sussex.

Rohase Piercy

Rohase Piercy was born in London in 1958, and now lives in Brighton on the South Coast of England with her husband Leslie and dog Spike. She has two grown-up daughters.

Also by Rohase Piercy

My Dearest Holmes

Before Elizabeth

A Case Of Domestic Pilfering
(with **Charlie Raven**)

For Children:
What Brave Bulls Do
(illustrated by **Nina Falaise**)

Rohase Piercy

Printed in Poland
by Amazon Fulfillment
Poland Sp. z o.o., Wrocław